BEATING ABOUT
THE BUSH

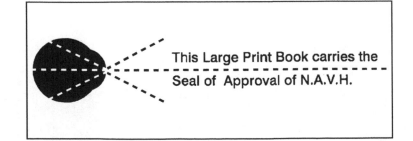

This Large Print Book carries the
Seal of Approval of N.A.V.H.

AN AGATHA RAISIN MYSTERY

BEATING ABOUT THE BUSH

M. C. BEATON

THORNDIKE PRESS
A part of Gale, a Cengage Company

Copyright © 2019 by M. C. Beaton.
Thorndike Press, a part of Gale, a Cengage Company.

Thorndike Press® Large Print Mystery
The text of this Large Print edition is unabridged.
Other aspects of the book may vary from the original edition.
Set in 16 pt. Plantin.

LIBRARY OF CONGRESS CIP DATA ON FILE.
CATALOGUING IN PUBLICATION FOR THIS BOOK
IS AVAILABLE FROM THE LIBRARY OF CONGRESS

ISBN-13: 978-1-4328-7139-0 (hardcover alk. paper)

Published in 2019 by arrangement with Macmillan Publishing Group, LLC/St. Martin's Press Publishing Group

Printed in Mexico
1 2 3 4 5 6 7 23 22 21 20 19

To all those avid readers who have kept up with Agatha over the years: it's because of you that she is now on her thirtieth sleuthing adventure! With love and thanks, Marion

CHAPTER ONE

Private detective Agatha Raisin was being driven back to her Cotswold home by her young and beautiful assistant Toni Gilmour. It was an early autumn evening and the sun briefly broke through a mantle of dark clouds to cast lengthening shadows across the road. They drove without conversation, the only sound the burble of the car's engine as it echoed off the embankments, trees, and hedgerows on either side of the country lane.

Agatha stole a glance towards Toni. She really was a very pretty young thing, she mused. Blonde hair, blue eyes, and a trim figure. Clothes were a bit cheap, and that short skirt had ridden up alarmingly while she had been driving. Decent legs, a bit skinny, not like Agatha's shapely, elegant pins. She cast an eye over her own exquisite grey Chanel suit, the skirt's hemline sitting just the right height above her knee. The jacket clung to her somewhat stocky frame in all the right places. She kept her figure in check with occasional bouts of furious dieting. She knew how to make the most of her assets. She could still show these youngsters a thing or two.

Who was she kidding? Toni was more than thirty years her junior. She didn't have to try to make the most of anything. At that age, she didn't have to try much at all. She just looked great. Agatha felt a sudden pang of jealousy.

"That skirt's a bit tarty for business, isn't it?" she said.

Toni shot her a look of exasperation. "Last time I wore it, you said it looked just right!" she said. "Or was that only because you wanted me playing the dumb blonde?"

"Be careful not to typecast yourself, dear," warned Agatha.

"You're impossible sometimes!" gasped Toni, her knuckles turning white as she clenched her fingers around the steering wheel.

Is she imagining those hands around my neck? wondered Agatha. In a rare moment of self-restraint, she bit her lip, deciding not to push Toni any further. She had felt waves of animosity emanating from the young woman all day and couldn't understand why. They had had a very successful day, after all. They were returning from a meeting with an engineering company, Morrison's, who had hired Raisin Investigations to look into what they believed to be industrial espionage.

The company manufactured batteries of various types and was developing a new battery pack that it claimed would double the range of an electric car. Strangers had been seen lurking around. There had even been a mysterious fire in the research and development department one night, although no one had been in the building at the time and the fire brigade could not be certain how the blaze had started. There was certainly no evidence to suggest arson.

Albert Morrison, the company's chairman, had signed a contract with Agatha before she and Toni had left his office, promising a very generous sum of money. Agatha had assured him that they would be on the case straightaway. The downside was that it would involve a lot of grunt work.

Any spy from a rival company hoping to steal Morrison's secrets would surely need help from someone on the inside. The investigation would entail trawling through employee records and conducting interviews, checking for anything unusual. They would be looking for anyone with a criminal background or serious money worries, or maybe someone harbouring some kind of grudge against the company. All that would mean working long hours, and those hours would have to be done by Agatha and Toni. Everyone else at the agency was up to their eyes in work. Divorce, it seemed, was the height of fashion these days, and it felt like half the married women in the county needed evidence of their husbands' philandering. Men seldom approached the agency to find evidence of their wives' infidelities. Most men seemed to prefer a more direct approach — confrontation and accusation. Women, Agatha believed, were more subtle, more cunning, more devious. The female of the species, as Kipling put it, is more deadly than the male.

Agatha's best detective, former policeman Patrick Mulligan, was not working on a divorce case but was bogged down on a surveillance job at Mircester's Isis Palace hotel, where the owners suspected that their manager was lining his pockets through various scams. Hanging around the hotel posing as a business executive, drinking at the bar, and eating in the restaurant was a job Agatha would have liked to take on herself, but the hotel wasn't exactly the

Savoy and the clientele gave her the creeps. The thought of sitting in the lounge fending off a series of sleazy sales reps was too tedious for words.

The only other member of staff not involved in adultery, unless he was sniffing around someone else's wife himself, was Simon Black. Agatha had sent him out prowling the streets of various villages every night, hot on the trail of the Cotswold Cat Strangler. The case was being funded by a concerned group of cat owners. She desperately wanted a result from Simon. She couldn't bear it that some nutcase was out there preying on poor innocent pets. She had never been much of an animal lover until she had acquired Hodge and Boswell, her own two cats, and she shuddered at the memory of when they had been kidnapped. Or would you say "catnapped"? No, that sounded like a nice, peaceful five-minute snooze. They had been taken when she was working on that case about those bloody bell ringers.

There was simply no one else available so, dreary though it was, the Morrison's job was down to Agatha and Toni. And it was going to be a long, hard slog if Toni's mood failed to improve.

What Agatha did not know was that Toni

11

had been dating a young medical student for some time. He had recently qualified as a doctor and was eager to get married. Toni was not in love with him, but she dearly wanted to have a stable home life. She longed to settle down and, eventually, have children. She knew Agatha would be dead set against any plan she might have that included marital bliss and a family on the horizon. She was bound to start interfering the moment she found out.

Toni knew very little about Agatha's upbringing, but she often suspected that it was not unlike her own — alcoholic parents bumbling through life in a haze of booze, barely acknowledging that they had a child, let alone caring for her. She frequently found herself looking upon Agatha as a mother figure. In turn, Agatha regularly rained on Toni's parade just like a real mother.

If Agatha found out about her young doctor, Toni was in no doubt that she would forecast that a marriage that did not start off with the newlyweds totally in love was doomed. Even those newlyweds who were utterly bursting with love didn't stand much of a chance in the long run. Suddenly everything about her boss irritated Toni, from her smoking to her whistling when she wasn't smoking. And every time they drove past thick undergrowth at the side of the road, did she *always* have to say "Nice place to dump a body"?

It was not as if Agatha herself set a particularly good example in the marriage stakes. Hadn't she become engaged to a man she barely knew and had met at Heathrow? And hadn't she cancelled the engagement a week later? Toni was convinced that her boss was actually in love with Sir Charles Fraith, her close friend and sometime lover. It was obvious that they were made for each other. Obvious to everyone, thought Toni, except Agatha and Sir Charles.

I'll keep *my* love life quiet, she vowed. But why does that decision make me feel guilty? Oh, here we go. She's looking at all that thick undergrowth on the left. The sun's just disappeared again. How can she hope to see anything in there in this gloom? Just for once, don't let her say it.

But she did.

"Nice place to dump a body."

"You always say that," snapped Toni, easing the car round a bend.

"STOP!" yelled Agatha.

Toni stamped on the brakes and the car screeched to a halt, pebbles spitting out from beneath the tyres.

"Back up," said Agatha.

Toni reversed and pulled into the side of the road. Agatha scrambled out of the car and began peering into the undergrowth. Toni was quickly by her side, squinting into the shadows.

"I don't see anything," she complained.

"There! Look there!"

She stared in the direction of Agatha's pointing finger. A thin shaft of light illuminated a foot in a sensible brogue.

"Maybe it's someone who fancied a kip," she said.

"In the middle of a thorny bush?" sneered Agatha. "I'd better look."

As Agatha moved towards the undergrowth, Toni turned her back, slipping her mobile phone out of her pocket. There was now every chance that she would be late for her date with her young doctor, and she needed to let him know.

"Aren't you coming?" demanded Agatha's voice at her elbow, making her jump. A faint flush of guilt coloured her cheeks as she crammed the phone back into her pocket.

"Lead on," she said.

"Who was that you were phoning?"

"A friend."

"Which one?"

"Mind your own business, Agatha. Let's

14

see if someone needs help in there."

Agatha pushed her way through thorny bramble bushes that tore at her tights. She grabbed at a low-hanging tree branch for balance, wobbling on high heels that were designed for traversing a cocktail lounge rather than a countryside ramble. She eased aside the higher tendrils of savage-looking vegetation to stop them from snagging on her jacket and hitched up her skirt to save it from being lacerated like her tights.

"That's really not a good look," said Toni.

"Well, you should know," Agatha replied, then froze. They were through the outer edge of the thicket, and only a few feet to their right they could see the brogue, the ankle, the lower leg, and . . . that was it. There was no body, just a sawn-off leg lying amid a litter of dead leaves and twigs. The sight of the dismembered limb sent a chill down Agatha's spine.

Toni backed away, tugging at her sleeve. "Back to the road and we'll phone the police. The killer may still be around." Numbly, Agatha followed her.

After they had called the police, they sat together in the car. Suddenly Toni said, "I know that foot."

Agatha looked at her and frowned. "How can you know a foot? You can know a man.

15

You can know a woman. You can know a person, but not a foot."

"I know whose foot it is," sighed Toni. "Saw it at Morrison's. Remember the woman who was on reception when we arrived to see the chairman? Mr. Albert, you know, the boss, he said something about seeing her in the morning. 'Secretary's afternoon off,' he said. I noticed her because she looked like a woman out of a forties dramatisation on telly. She was wearing a tweed jacket and skirt, and ribbed woollen stockings, and those brogues."

Agatha did remember the woman. She had looked strangely out of place. Morrison's was supposed to be a twenty-first-century hi-tech company, and having a relic like her to greet potential clients had struck Agatha as a mistake.

"No stocking," she said. "Maybe not her."

"Maybe whoever did it took off the stocking when they sawed the leg off."

"Why? And why only one leg?" demanded Agatha. "In fact, why a leg at all? I mean, you read about hands being cut off and teeth removed to stop identification, but why a leg? Oh, snakes and bastards. I *am* going to smoke."

"Why don't you vape?" asked Toni.

"Why don't you roll down the window or

16

go for a walk?" snapped Agatha.

She watched Toni walk a little way away from the car before she lit up a cigarette. Then her eyes narrowed. Toni was phoning someone. She was smiling. In the growing dusk, her face looked almost luminous. She looked happy, mellow, bordering on serene. Alarm bells were ringing for Agatha. Had the silly girl gone and fallen in love? Of course, it might not be love, she thought; she might have won the lottery. I'd rather she won the lottery than fall in love with some fellow and get married. That would be disastrous. She's the only one who can run the agency when I'm away.

She heard police sirens approaching and stubbed out her cigarette. She got out of the car and joined Toni, who immediately switched off her phone. The scene on the darkening, hedge-flanked road, already sinister, took on an even more eerie appearance when the thorny foliage was frozen in the flickering blue lights of the first police car.

"Where is it?" asked the policeman who stepped out of the car.

"Over there," said Agatha. "Oh, it gets dark so quickly. You can't see it from here now. I'll show you."

He was joined by another policeman.

"Name?" said the first one.

"Don't you want to look at the leg?"

"It's like this. Forensics will be along and they'll say we've trampled all over a crime scene."

"But what if a fox or something drags it away while we're waiting?" wailed Agatha.

"Now then, you've had a shock. Name and address?"

At that moment, Detective Sergeant Bill Wong arrived accompanied by Detective Alice Peterson. Bill was a long-time friend and Alice was his fiancée as well as his colleague. Agatha begged them to look at the leg.

"I was just telling this here woman," said the policeman, "that it don't do to muck up a crime scene before Forensics —"

"All right," snapped Bill. "We'll suit up."

Agatha waited impatiently while Bill and Alice struggled into their forensic suits and boots. When they pulled hoods over their heads and masks onto their faces, they became two anonymous creatures in white. As they headed into the undergrowth, there were more sirens, more blue lights, and an ambulance arrived, followed by an unmarked police car. The road was now completely blocked and officers were marking the crime scene, rolling out miles of blue-and-white tape. Traffic was starting to queue outside the taped cordon. Agatha, forbidden by the police to leave the side of the road, was shouting instructions to Bill when, from the unmarked car, there emerged the unmistakable figure of Chief Inspector Wilkes.

"You again," he said through clenched teeth. "I might have known."

"Shh!" hissed Agatha. "They're getting close."

Silence. Thin, cold rain began to fall. A forensic team arrived. When they too had suited up, they walked into the undergrowth and headed for the gleam of Bill's torch. An owl sailed overhead. Agatha Raisin lit a cigarette and fretted. What on earth were they doing?

Suddenly Bill erupted from the undergrowth, branches tearing at the flimsy fabric of his forensic suit.

"Agatha," he said, "this is some sort of joke. The leg is a fake."

"I thought — Ouch!" Toni exclaimed. Agatha had begun to shake and had burnt the back of Toni's hand with her cigarette.

"Sorry, dear," she said. "Nerves."

"You thought what?" demanded Bill.

"I thought I knew that foot," said Toni.

Sirens sounded in the distance. More police were arriving. "Knew that foot? How

19

can you know a foot?" demanded the chief inspector.

"Mrs. Dinwiddy, the secretary to the chairman at Morrison's. She wore brogues like that, and wool stockings. I remember wondering about those stockings and thought she might have an allergy to synthetic fabrics."

"This is typical of your amateur theatrics," roared Wilkes, storming back to his car. "Sergeant, get this lot out of here and get this road opened again. And you two," he added, turning to Agatha and Toni, "are lucky I'm not charging you with wasting police time!"

Bill Wong looked at Agatha, sighed, and shook his head.

"You have to admit," said Agatha, "that from a distance it did look like a —"

"Just drop it, Agatha," he said, tugging at his now grubby and shredded white suit.

Agatha flopped into the passenger seat and slammed the car door. She looked down at her tights, dragged, snagged, and ruined, and brushed raindrops and hedgerow debris off her jacket and skirt. They would have to go to the dry cleaner's, or possibly the bin.

"It did look real," she said.

"It looked exactly like Mrs. Dinwiddy's,"

20

agreed Toni.

"But didn't we leave her back at Morrison's?"

"No. She left after handing over the typed contracts, remember? Her afternoon off. Said she had to go to the hospital in Mircester to see her sick sister. We stayed to sign the contracts and discuss how we would tackle the case. Then you insisted on telling Albert Morrison all about your whole long list of successful cases, and as you know, that can take forever."

"That was a bitchy remark!" said Agatha.

A rap at the car window interrupted the conversation. A police constable, his hat dripping with rainwater, motioned for her to wind the window down. They were going to have to make detailed statements.

It was to be the beginning of a long evening of questioning. Agatha's only comforting thought was that word would spread quickly, as it always did in this neck of the woods. She was also pretty sure she had seen a reporter lurking by the roadside outside the cordon. The incident was so ludicrous that it was bound to make the local press. All of that meant that Charles would soon hear about it and come running, as he had done so many times before.

■ ■ ■ ■

Few words passed between Agatha and Toni as they drove to Carsely. Turning off the A44, they cruised down into the village, which sheltered in a dip, hidden away in the Cotswold Hills. Passing the church and the line of shops and terraced stone houses in the high street, Agatha told Toni to turn into Lilac Lane and drop her right outside her garden gate at the end of the straggle of cottages. Even in the darkened lane, she was loath to be seen in her current bedraggled state — and in Carsely there was always someone watching.

"Agatha . . ." said Toni as she got out of the car. "I wondered . . ."

"What?" Agatha really didn't want to hang around.

The whole truth and nothing but the truth means no rendezvous with the young doctor tonight, thought Toni. She'll drag me inside for a lecture that could go on for hours. Best stick to the work bit. "There was no sun," she said. "No setting sun to shine on that leg. I think some hoaxer was holding a torch."

"The world is full of nutters," said Agatha. "See you tomorrow."

22

But as she swiftly opened her front door and slipped into her cramped hallway, she thought: who would know that we would drive past on that road at that time?

Agatha and Toni were in the Raisin Investigations office, above an antique shop in one of the oldest lanes of central Mircester, when Toni eventually brought Agatha up to speed with her police statement. Agatha was leaning against the front of her over-large pseudo-Georgian desk while Toni hovered near the door, a sheaf of papers in her hand.

In her statement, Toni had laid out the whole story of their afternoon at Morrison's. They had been given lunch in the directors' dining room. At one point, Agatha had excused herself and gone to the loo. A young man, John Sayer, head of human resources, had asked Toni if Agatha was a good boss. Toni had praised Agatha but had said she was anxious to get away on time that evening because she had a date, and Agatha sometimes drove slowly, peering at the undergrowth at the side of the road and saying "Nice place to dump a body." And that on a couple of occasions she had been sure she had seen something and had insisted Toni leave the car and search through the trees and bushes with her.

"You put that in your statement?" said Agatha. "You told him I said that?"

"You say it all the time."

"I DO NOT say it all the time!"

"Yes you do. It's one of your worst habits."

"I DO NOT have . . . *habits*!" Agatha snarled.

Toni put the index finger and forefinger of her right hand to her mouth, pulled them away, and exhaled through pursed lips as though blowing out smoke.

"Smoking is not a habit," said Agatha. "It is a therapeutic aid to rational, logical thought. Not that you could be expected to know anything about that!"

Toni then had to endure a lecture about loyalty, dedication, duty, reliability, and how a trustworthy confidante never, ever talks about friends behind their backs.

"Haven't I been good to you?" demanded Agatha.

"Spare me the guilt trip," said Toni. "This is a good time to tell you. I want to have a personal life. I need a bit of time to myself."

"You've got it!" raged Agatha. "To think of all the times I have looked after you. Why, if it weren't for me, you'd be —"

"Oh, shut your stupid face!" yelled Toni. "You want my resignation?"

"No, she doesn't," came a pleasant mascu-

24

line voice from the top of the stairs.

"Charles!" cried Agatha, recognising the voice of Sir Charles Fraith. "Where have you been?"

"I thought you might need some comfort after I read the *Mircester Mail* this morning."

Charles sauntered past Toni into the office. "Get me a coffee, Toni," said Agatha, dismissing the younger woman with a wave of her hand.

"Get it yourself," snapped Toni.

"I will speak to you later," said Agatha. "Let's go to the pub, Charles. I am weary and don't feel like coping with Toni's tantrums."

They crossed the lane and settled into two armchairs at a table inside the latticed window of the King Charles.

"What on earth came over Toni?" said Agatha. "I only gave her a mild ticking-off."

"You never give anyone a mild ticking-off. You are a fault-finder supreme. Out with it."

Agatha described how Toni had gossiped about Agatha's propensity to remark "Nice place to dump a body" almost every time they were on the road. Clearly some prankster had put the leg there in the hope that she would spot it and be made to look like a complete fool.

"You do, as a matter of fact," said Charles. "Not look like a complete fool. I mean, you do say that thing about a nice place to dump a body. But I'm sure you reminded Toni of all she owed you, and no one likes emotional blackmail, so she became furious as well. I sometimes think you don't value people enough. You often bark commands at me as if I'm one of your detectives. And what did your Heathrow Romeo think when you dumped him after a week?"

"I neither know nor care," said Agatha. "The man was intolerable. He wanted me to travel the world with him like we were on one long, endless holiday. What sort of madness is that? *He* may have decided to retire and travel, but I have far more life left in me than that. I have a business to run, employees, responsibilities."

"Really," said Charles, nodding. Agatha could tell by that flicker of a smile at the corner of his mouth that he knew she wasn't actually telling him the truth. He would wait, and they both knew that she would tell him eventually. Right now, she wasn't prepared to admit that she had plunged herself into an engagement with a man whom she very quickly discovered had a

26

string of other fiancées around the world — Stella in New York, Carrie in Cape Town, Barbara in Brisbane. And those were only the three she had found out about. There were bound to be more. He must have been buying diamond engagement rings in bulk. Well, he could keep hers. She'd shoved it in his ear while he was recovering from a ferocious slap in the face, before she kicked him out the front door.

"Yes, really," she said. "And oh, look! The ice is melting in my gin. I'm talking too much. Let me take a couple of sips."

"Knock yourself out."

Silence. Then a sniffle.

"Are you crying?" asked Charles. "This will never do, Aggie. Here, take this." He reached inside his jacket and produced a perfectly folded pristine white handkerchief. A linen handkerchief. Who the hell carried linen handkerchiefs nowadays? Most men would struggle to find a crumpled used paper tissue in the bottom of some disgusting trouser pocket, thought Agatha, dabbing her tears. But Sir Charles Fraith was not most men.

From behind the crisp linen, her bear-like brown eyes studied his movements, not for the first time, as he rose to his feet. He moved with an effortless grace. His sports jacket hung faithfully from his shoulders, as though it would fit no other, which, of course, it wouldn't. It had been hand-tailored for him. His cavalry twill trousers were casual but untroubled by any sign of crumpling. Charles was a crease-free zone. The bottom of his trouser legs sat lazily on the lacing of his brown Oxford shoes. They were polished but not too shiny. Ideal for country wear. No gentleman would wear brown shoes in town. Town, of course, meant his London club, not a back-street pub in Mircester.

Charles would have emerged from that leg-incident bramble thicket looking like he had just stepped out of his Savile Row tailor's, unlike Agatha, who had looked like she'd been spat out by a combine harvester. Even when they had clambered over walls together to break into a monastery in the Pyrenees in search of her ex-husband, he never had a thread out of place. If he were ever — perish the thought — to grow wrinkly with age, Gustav, his loyal retainer, would find a way to iron him.

"Got to pee," he said. "Back in a minute."

He seemed to be gone a long time. Agatha reached for her handbag to find her cigarettes, then remembered that smoking had been banned in English pubs for more

28

than a decade. She fidgeted with the clasp on the bag, swirled the last of the ice in her glass and looked up to see Charles walking back into the bar. He was not alone. Toni was at his shoulder.

"What's *she* doing here?" demanded Agatha.

"Toni is here," explained Charles calmly, "because, odd as it may seem, ladies, I am becoming interested in this case. I'd like to know what's going on, and for that, I need both of you. So begin at the beginning and go on to the end."

It was Toni who began summing up. She explained that they rarely came across cases of industrial espionage, and this one appeared to be something they could really get their teeth into. Like a dry, dull, and boring church fête sponge cake, thought Agatha, but she said nothing, letting Toni continue. Someone, it would appear, rated their abilities highly enough to plant that dummy sawn-off leg in the undergrowth for them to find. "So," said Toni, "maybe someone wants us to look like fools and discredit us. Maybe whoever it was will try to trip us up again, forcing Morrison's to terminate our contract and hire someone else."

"That," said Agatha, nodding in agreement, "might buy them some time to finish whatever moves they are making against Morrison's. But going so far as to make it look like the secretary's leg is bizarre. I think that's someone not only clever but quite mad."

"It need not have been someone in Morrison's office who heard me talking to John Sayer," pondered Toni. "Just someone who bugged the place."

"It's all to do with an electric car battery pack this firm has invented," said Agatha. "They say it can give a car more miles than any others on the market, and that will be worth a fortune. Burning down the research and development department must have set the project back months."

"There were seven people in the room when I made that remark about Agatha," said Toni. "I will look into their histories tomorrow."

"We'll both do that," said Agatha, and then suddenly smiled at her assistant. "Truce?"

"Truce," said Toni.

How to describe that smile of Agatha's without falling into cliché? wondered Charles. It lights up the room? It lights up your life? It melts your heart? He gave a

30

mental shrug. Just be grateful the storm has passed.

"Must rush," said Toni. "Pick you up at eight thirty tomorrow morning."

Toni was silent as she drove Agatha to the factory in the morning. The previous evening her young doctor had seemed, for the first time, rather dull. She had felt pretty flat throughout the entire time they had spent together at his place. He had cooked a dreadfully bland risotto. She had gone home early, weary and listless. Was it him? Was it her? Or was it just the risotto?

Agatha broke the silence as Toni pulled into the car park by saying, "I wonder what's next?"

"Maybe another body part," said Toni. "I think he's mocking us."

"Could be a woman," said Agatha. "Come on, Toni, I need you to be thinking straight." Then she paused. "I am really quite concerned about you."

Toni stiffened. "If you are going to poke into my private life, Agatha, forget it."

"I didn't know there was anything to poke into," said Agatha, then swiftly changed tack back to the case. "If this character is as mad as I think he is, he'll play little tricks for a while, but then cruelty will take over his twisted brain and you might be the target."

"Or you."

Agatha gave a little shiver. "Whichever one of us he thinks is the most vulnerable."

"I brought the bug-sweeping kit," said Toni. "I suggest I do the conference room first."

Agatha climbed slowly out of the car and scowled. This new stiffness in her joints *couldn't* be age. Maybe it was that damned car seat. Yes, that must be it. She never felt stiff and old when she got out of Charles's BMW.

At the reception desk, Mrs. Dinwiddy was there to greet them — tweed suit, pearls, wool stockings, and brogues. In her left hand she held a small dictation recorder, its strap looped around her wrist. She seemed anxious to get back to her work as she briskly escorted them to the conference room, which had been set aside for their use. Agatha stood in silence, staring out of the window, while Toni worked her way methodically around the room holding something that looked like an old-fashioned transistor radio. The gadget could detect any kind of recording equipment, transmitter or hidden camera. She moved it this way and that, sweeping it over the walls, skirting boards, furniture, and light fittings. She finished with the dark oak conference table and its centrepiece decoration of two odd-looking ornamental antique ashtrays.

Agatha scrutinised the factory buildings. It was a surprisingly small complex that must originally have been farm steadings. They had been converted and extended many years before, probably around the 1950s, in Agatha's estimation. Paint was peeling from window frames and guttering hung loose here and there. On the other side of a courtyard stood what must have been the research and development department, now little more than a shell. The autumn wind soughed and moaned round the stone buildings. At some point, someone had attempted to grow flowers and bushes, but over the years the planting had degenerated into a tangle of trees and undergrowth. Over the bending trees, curtsying in the wind, ragged clouds chased across a pale grey sky.

"We're clear," said Toni, slotting the scanner back into its black plastic case.

"Then let's get to work," said Agatha.

On the table in front of them were piles of manila folders stuffed with documents. The first pile was the smallest — the six people who might have overheard Toni talking to John Sayer. Sayer's file was on top.

After they had been sifting through the files for what seemed like hours, Mrs. Dinwiddy arrived with coffee. She placed it on the table in front of them with barely a word and swiftly made her exit. Agatha was raising a cup to her lips when Toni suddenly shouted, "Don't drink it!"

Agatha lowered the cup. "Why?"

"A hunch. Not poison. Some sort of laxative."

"A lax—" Agatha squirmed in her seat. "We need a guinea pig." The door opened and Mrs. Dinwiddy returned.

"I have been told to ask if you ladies need anything further."

"Try this coffee," said Agatha.

"I never drink coffee, Mrs. Raisin. But if you think it is substandard in any way, I will bring you a fresh pot. I also have two lunch tickets for you for the executive dining room, on this floor at the end of the corridor and turn left. Today is toad in the hole. That is a particular favourite of our chairman, Mr. Albert."

"Yuck," said Agatha after the secretary had left.

"I like sausages," said Toni, "so it's okay with me."

"Why do you think the coffee might be spiked with a laxative?"

"Because I keep thinking of a childish, twisted sort of brain. A laxative could leave us both . . . well . . . indisposed in a most undignified way. Once again, we could be made a laughing stock."

At lunch, Toni pronounced the toad in the hole to be excellent, and Agatha had to agree that the sausages in golden batter were delicious. This was followed by Icky Sticky pudding, as heavy as it sounded, and both felt sleepy afterwards, wishing that they hadn't eaten so much. Agatha was in no doubt that she was wishing harder than Toni, mainly because the tightness of the waistband of her skirt was depressing her.

The police seemed to have dismissed the whole dummy leg affair as a practical joke. Not one policeman had turned up at the factory to follow up on it, or so Mrs. Dinwiddy had assured them.

Agatha tried to concentrate on the personnel files in front of her, but her mind kept wandering. The tyranny of words. One didn't say "personnel" any more. One said "human resources." Honestly! In the future, children would be yelling "Personnel!" in the playground and being smacked for using a dirty word. Only smacking had also been banned, hadn't it? Probably a good thing, although she could think of a few people who could do with a slap. In fact, the more she thought about it, the longer the list became. Her lying swine of an ex-fiancé was still sitting right at the top. The image of Charles's hurt face, lit by the glare of a street light as he stood on the pavement peering in at her engagement party to which he had not been invited, filled her mind. Snakes and bastards! Concentrate!

What was this? Her eyes suddenly focused on the file in front of her. Jennifer Williams, aged twenty-eight; previous occupation, trapeze artist. That was odd. Circus people hardly ever did anything else but work for the circus. Agatha phoned Mrs. Dinwiddy and asked if it would be possible to interview Jennifer Williams.

"She works in the packing department," said Mrs. Dinwiddy. "If she is in the building, I will send her to you."

Agatha told Toni why she had summoned the girl, and when the door opened and a young woman was ushered in, they both looked at her curiously. "Miss Williams," announced Mrs. Dinwiddy, giving her a little push into the room.

One reason Jennifer Williams might no longer be a trapeze artist was immediately apparent. She had a large, round face and several chins. Her bosoms were like pillows and her hips were so large they formed cliffs on either side of her body, from which her enormous black skirt hung. She had tight black curly hair. Round the back it looked as if a family of circus dwarves might have set up camp in the garment, Agatha thought.

"We were searching through the staff files for anomalies," began Agatha.

"I'm British, me. No anomi-whatsits in our family."

"I mean, you worked in a circus. Why did you leave?"

"He dropped me, see. Near broke my neck."

"Who did?"

"Cousin Alfie. Said I'd got too heavy. Said one o' me sequins had popped off and near blinded him. Me dad works with the horses. Did he take my part? Naw! Said I had to start losing weight. Always fancied a job here. Canteen's the best for miles around."

"Do you get on well with your colleagues?" asked Agatha.

"Mostly," replied Jennifer, "though there's a few as thinks they're a cut above the likes of me. That dozy tart on reception for one."

"On reception?" said Toni. "Do you mean Mrs. Dinwiddy?"

"Not her," smiled Jennifer. "The one that

got sacked. The young blonde girl, although Din-whatsit's as bad. Everyone knows she's only here because she's keepin' the boss's batteries charged with a bit of rumpy-pumpy, if you know what I mean."

"Mrs. Dinwiddy is having an affair with Albert Morrison?" Agatha was incredulous.

"You didn't hear that from me!" said Jennifer. "I ain't sayin' no more. I likes workin' here. Don't want to lose me job. We got shepherd's pie on Thursday."

Agatha dismissed the former trapeze artist, who waddled out of the room.

"Interesting snippet of gossip there," Toni said. "Morrison and Dinwiddy? Really?"

"Gossip is exactly what it sounds like to me," said Agatha. "It's scarcely believable, but worth bearing in mind. He is a married man, so I suppose that might give his wife, or even Dinwiddy, a grudge against him and his company. And what happened to that young receptionist? We need to know why she was sacked."

"We should really set the files aside now," said Toni, "and interview the people who were in the room when I made that unfortunate remark."

Biting down a sudden, almost liverish desire to quarrel with her assistant again, Agatha sighed and agreed.

Those who had been present amounted to six people and the chairman, Albert Morrison. But before any of them could arrive to be interviewed, Mrs. Dinwiddy barged in.

"I believe you want to know how many people heard the young lady's remark about Mrs. Raisin talking about good places to hide bodies," she said. "I am afraid most of the building was privy to it. Mr. Morrison believes in an open-office policy. You are in one of the only rooms shielded from the staff. Discussions of any kind are broadcast to everyone. It is based on a Japanese model that Mr. Morrison admired when he visited that country last year."

"Thank you," replied Agatha bleakly. When the secretary had left, she said, "If only it had been a genuine leg. Then the whole police force would be on it and at least we could pick up some crumbs of information." She lit a cigarette and blew a cloud of smoke up to the fluorescent lighting.

"You can't smoke in here, Agatha."

"Who says?"

"Everybody says."

"Screw everybody."

A smoke alarm she had failed to notice went off above her head with a deafening screech. She clambered up on the table and, teetering on her high heels, flapped a handkerchief, the one Charles had lent her, at the gadget. Stepping sideways for balance, she planted one of her heels in her half-full coffee cup. The awful sound slowly died away, but when she pulled her foot free of the cup and shook it to dry it, she overbalanced and toppled off the table onto the floor.

The door opened and a man in overalls walked in. He strode past Agatha, climbed onto the table and removed the smoke alarm. "Orders are you can now smoke." Then he jumped down and left, leaving a bemused Agatha, still lying on the floor, staring after him.

Toni ran round to help her boss to her feet.

"This is creepy," said Agatha, sinking gratefully into a chair. She dried her foot with her handkerchief. "I could do with a drink."

"There's a pub not too far along the main road," said Toni. "And you're right, this place *is* creepy. Full of weirdos. Why didn't that man help you up? Odd."

"Let's get out of here," said Agatha, and they headed for the pub.

CHAPTER TWO

The pub was just under a mile from the factory entrance. It looked like a comfortable, slightly ramshackle country inn, yet it clearly wasn't as old as its blackened wooden beams would have you believe. It had been built in the 1930s, when there had been a fashion for architecture with fake Tudor embellishments. Swinging lazily in the afternoon breeze was a badly weathered pub sign with cracked and peeling paint portraying a merry peasant in a smock dancing with a pig. It forlornly announced the establishment as the Jolly Farmer. Toni pulled into the car park. Apart from a rusting truck, there were no other vehicles in sight. This was clearly not a busy time.

Inside, the low ceilings of the pub were dressed with yet more fake beams. The walls were adorned with tarnished horse brasses alongside old photographs of miserable peasants scowling at the camera and, therefore, at Agatha. She scowled back. Unlike so many other pubs scattered across the Cotswold countryside, the Jolly Farmer had allowed the growing trend for serving good, tasty food to pass it by. No effort had been made to attract a regular following amongst either local foodies or the tourist trade. For those customers driven to foolhardy bravery by desperate hunger, a large jar of pickled eggs stood on the counter beside a glass case displaying a small selection of limp sandwiches.

"What a dump," muttered Agatha, who then noticed the barman smiling at her from behind the lager taps and said in a louder voice, "Very quiet in here."

The barman was a small, dapper man, more like an accountant or some sort of clerk than a pub landlord. His voice was high and reedy. "What will be your pleasure, ladies? Yes, it is quiet. But we do often get the odd alky before the evening rush."

Agatha blinked. She had a sudden vision of herself leaning over the bar, grabbing the little man by the throat and shouting, "Are you calling me an alcoholic?" Instead she said, "A gin and tonic. Make it a double. What are you having, Toni?"

"I'll have an orange juice."

They carried their drinks over to a table

in front of a fire of glowing fake logs that gave off no heat. They glowed only because they were illuminated by an electric bulb. The table was meant to resemble a tree stump. There was a toadstool lamp in the middle.

"I feel like Alice in Wonderland," said Toni.

"Well it wouldn't surprise me if we turned up a Mad Hatter at Morrison's," said Agatha. "I mean, that man who zipped in, dismantled the smoke alarm, and zipped out again without even offering me a hand wasn't exactly normal, was he?"

"And then there's the trapeze artist," said Toni, "and that Dinwiddy woman. None of the staff we've met so far are what you would call normal."

"They are not," Agatha agreed, "but none of them seem like spies or saboteurs either. First rule in the spy game is to blend in, don't attract attention. I sense there's a twisted mind at work here. Someone really clever and utterly ruthless. We could spend weeks going through the files and not find a thing."

"What I find odd," said Toni, "is why that trapeze girl was employed in the first place. I mean, you don't need the brightest of workers packing boxes, but there are plenty of people out there looking for jobs. Why take on someone who clearly has problems?"

"Maybe her circus training gave her quick hands," Agatha joked. "She might pack boxes faster than anyone else. We need to find out if what she said about the receptionist is true, though. We need to talk to the man who does the hiring and firing."

"John Sayer," said Toni. "Human resources. Better get a move on. Sayer told me that the factory workers are on shifts right round the clock, but most of the clerical staff leave at five thirty."

Agatha finished her drink. "Right, let's go."

"Oh, leaving so soon?" came the reedy voice of the barman. Agatha cast him a withering look and was about to say something along the lines of "Not soon enough" when he piped up again. "Not you. The young one. Haven't seen a good-looking blonde in here for weeks."

"And you never will if they see you first, you nasty little man," snarled Agatha.

Toni seized her arm and all but dragged her from the pub. "Honestly, Agatha. You are getting worse. You never used to be so bad-tempered all the time."

"I AM NOT BAD-TEMPERED!" Agatha got into the passenger seat of Toni's small car and lit up a cigarette. Wait a minute. What had that sleazy creep said? Toni had just turned the key in the ignition when Agatha flung open the door and clambered out.

"I'll be back in a minute," she said, striding towards the pub door.

Toni clasped the top of the steering wheel and rested her head on the backs of her hands. What on earth was her boss up to this time? She could never keep her nose out of trouble.

"Couldn't stay away, eh?" trilled the barman as Agatha walked in. "Where's the pretty one?"

"She's outside being blonde," smiled Agatha through gritted teeth. "Can't find the car keys."

"Like a drink while you're waiting?" the barman asked.

"No thank you," said Agatha, "but I was interested in what you said about blondes. I'm . . . er . . . involved in compiling a survey for . . . um . . . *Lovely Locks,* the hair fashion magazine. They say blondes are a disappearing breed — an endangered species, so to speak. You said you hadn't seen one for weeks?"

"Nope," said the barman. "Not since Josie went off to travel the world."

"Josie?" said Agatha. "Was she a regular?"

"Fairly regular. She worked on reception at Morrison's. Came in after work from time to time. She'd have a couple and then head back to the factory."

"Why would they need a receptionist at night?"

"Oh, I don't believe young Josie spent none of her night shifts on reception," twittered the barman with a leer. "More like on her back . . . on a couch in the boss's office! Now, if that lovely daughter of yours has lost her keys, maybe you should phone for help and bring her back inside."

"She is NOT my daughter," Agatha assured him. "And if in any doubt, a gentleman would have said 'sister.' "

"Ah, but it's plain she ain't that," said the barman. "You're too long in the tooth and broad in the beam to have a tasty youngster like that for a sister."

"I've changed my mind," said Agatha. "I will have a drink after all."

"What will it be?"

"A pint of lager."

She slapped some cash on the counter as the barman poured the golden liquid into a tall glass.

"Wouldn't have had you down as a lager drinker," he said.

46

"I'm not," said Agatha, "but it has its uses." She picked up the pint, poured it over the barman's head, and stomped out.

As Agatha and Toni drew up at the gates to Morrison's, a gaggle of factory girls bustled past, heading down the main road towards Mircester, a few minutes' walk away.

"So Albert Morrison was sleeping with Josie?" said Toni.

"I doubt they did much sleeping," said Agatha, watching the girls go by and wondering if Morrison had tried it on with any of them as well. "And if she was his bit on the side, why would he get rid of her? We're going to have to be very careful who we question about this and what we ask if we want to get to the truth."

She peered through the windscreen at the factory buildings. The lights were on, the Cotswold stone walls glowing yellow near the windows, but gradually submitting to the grey of the gathering evening gloom further from the light. Suddenly the old farm steadings, despite their sympathetic extensions, looked remarkably small.

"And another thing," she said, as Toni eased the car through the gates. "This place isn't very big. I mean, if they are producing batteries, we should have heard machinery operating, shouldn't we? How big are these batteries? We need to know more about what's going on here."

They were halfway up the short, shrub-lined approach to the factory when Agatha cried, "Stop!"

Toni looked uneasily into the bushes on either side, but saw nothing. "What?" she asked.

"There's no guard on the gate," said Agatha. "There are supposed to be two, aren't there? One who does nights and one who does days. For an organisation that's paranoid about industrial espionage, they're not taking security very seriously."

They parked the car outside the entrance to the main building and walked in to find Mrs. Dinwiddy sitting at the reception desk.

"I understand that you decamped to a public house," she said disapprovingly. "Well, it's too late for you to talk to anyone now. As you can see, it's five thirty and the workforce has left for the night."

"We were told that only the clerical staff left at five thirty," said Agatha. "The factory workforce operates in shifts, twenty-four hours a day."

"Yes, but not here," tutted Mrs. Dinwiddy, adjusting the wristband from which dangled her dictation recorder. "How could you think we made anything here? This is our head office, but its function is mainly administrative. Yes, we have a packing and dispatch department to send out small orders and samples, but there is no manufacturing facility here."

"Where *is* the factory?" asked Agatha.

"It's in Sekiliv. Eastern Europe. Other side of Poland. No trouble with unions. Cheap labour."

"And have you started production of the battery pack for electric cars?"

"Not yet. Our other products are still being manufactured, but the fire in the research and development department has delayed the new electric car pack."

"The fire seems more than a mere delay," said Agatha. "I've seen the R&D building. It was gutted."

"Development is continuing nevertheless. That work is now being undertaken in Sekiliv."

"Why were we not told about Sekiliv?" said Agatha, a tone of sceptical frustration creeping into her voice. "In fact, why have we never been offered a tour of the premises here? How can we be expected to do our job if we're not fully in the picture —"

"Mrs. Dinwiddy," Toni interrupted, anxious to avoid any kind of row, "we are very curious about the business of the leg in the bushes."

"A practical joke at your expense, no doubt," said Mrs. Dinwiddy.

"No doubt," agreed Toni, "but aren't you a little concerned that someone tried to make it look like *your* leg? I mean, why go to that trouble? Could it be that someone is trying to frighten you? Someone with a grudge against you?"

Mrs. Dinwiddy gave a surprisingly girlish laugh. Agatha studied the small wrinkles at the corners of her eyes, the crease at the side of her mouth. She saw a faint flush appear on the receptionist's cheeks and suddenly realised that, apart from a rudimentary smear of lipstick, Mrs. Dinwiddy was wearing no make-up. This woman, she thought, doesn't do herself any favours with her drab dress, her comfortable shoes, her frumpy hairstyle, and her lack of essential investment in cosmetics, but she is probably no older than me. If necessary, Agatha would admit to being in her early fifties; younger if a combination of recent diet, flattering haute couture, and gin made it seem achievable. Mrs. Dinwiddy, she mused, might not be the dowdy widow they had assumed her to be. But was she the merry widow who bedded the boss? That stretched

50

the imagination further than the trapeze girl's knicker elastic.

"Members of staff sometimes tease me," said Mrs. Dinwiddy calmly. She looked Toni up and down with hard eyes. "Immature young women can be so thoughtless and cruel."

Toni shifted uncomfortably.

"There are times, at office functions when they have drunk more than is good for them, and places, such as when they go gossiping in corridors, when they let their stupid mouths run away with them. They say more than they should. That is why I always carry this." She held up her slim little electronic dictation machine. "I record their vicious tittle-tattle and play it to them the following day. They know that if I ever hear them utter another word, I will play the recording to Mr. Albert."

Mrs. Dinwiddy normally had a face as bland as her clothing, with no strong feature, no remarkable aspect, but with her last remark, it was as if it had grown bones of malice. The eyes narrowed, the mouth became trap-like.

"In other words," said Agatha, "you know where the bodies are buried."

"In a manner of speaking," said the secretary. "The security guard is waiting to lock

51

up. Please leave."

"Mrs. Dinwiddy," said Toni, "the leg we found had a brogue on it just like yours. Can you think of an explanation?"

"Not really . . . Oh dear. Of course! I keep a spare pair of shoes in my locker. You see, during the floods last year, we had to wade through a sort of lake to get into the office. I'll go and look."

Mrs. Dinwiddy's sensible low heels pounded the dull linoleum on the floor of the corridor leading away from the reception desk. There was silence as she barged through the door into the staff locker room. A murmur of wind wafted round the building. Then she came clumping back. "They've gone! How very odd."

Agatha exchanged a glance with Toni. There might now be a way to begin narrowing down the list of suspects for the false leg prank. And that might shed some light on the industrial espionage affair.

"We need to talk to John Sayer," Agatha said. "We will have to look at attendance records and work rotas to help us determine who might have had the opportunity to leave here and plant the leg in a place where I was sure to spot it."

"Yes, yes," said Mrs. Dinwiddy, pulling on her coat and looking over her shoulder, "but

Mr. Sayer has left for the evening and the guard is coming. He will want us all out. You will have to come back tomorrow."

Agatha prided herself on giving credit where credit was due, and as they walked to Toni's car, she said, "That was smart of you. I really should have thought more about why it was Mrs. Dinwiddy's leg — fake leg — left in the undergrowth."

"I find her a bit intimidating," said Toni. "Those pale eyes of hers have a sort of blind look, and then when they suddenly focus . . . well, it's like some shark thingummy sighting its prey."

"I'm usually the one who notices things like that," said Agatha. "I mean, I am sensitive to all that kind of thing. Hypersensitive, in fact."

Usually, thought Toni, you are as sensitive as a charging rhino. Then, as though to confound her, Agatha proved that she was indeed capable of picking up subtle pointers.

"That Dinwiddy woman may be intimidating," she said, "but she didn't want to have anything to do with the security guard, did she? She couldn't wait to get out before he came prowling round."

"We definitely need to have a word with the guards tomorrow," said Toni.

"Agreed," said Agatha. "Now, you may drive me straight home. I don't feel like going into the office."

"Is James back from his travels?"

James Lacey, Agatha's ex-husband, was also her neighbour. "I neither know nor care," she said. He had left without calling round to say goodbye, which she regarded as a slight, conveniently forgetting all the times she had gone abroad without stopping for a moment to think of even telling him where she was going. And he had not been there when she had needed help during a recent escapade in Bulgaria. What was the point of having an ex-husband who was a former soldier and travel writer if he wasn't there when you needed him on a foreign mission? James had been fussing over his divorce from his far-too-young, far-too-beautiful, and far-too-dim Croatian wife. It was Charles who had been there for her. Charles was dependable, in his own unpredictable way. He was inconsistently dependable. Could anyone be that? If anyone could, thought Agatha, it was Charles.

The following morning, Agatha and Toni arrived at Morrison's bright and early and were escorted to the conference room by

Mrs. Dinwiddy, wearing her usual unremarkable neutral attire and unremarkable neutral expression. She was polite but made no mention of their conversation the previous evening. Agatha asked to see John Sayer, and Mrs. Dinwiddy assured her that Mr. Sayer was already aware of her request for an interview and would attend the conference room shortly. Just as she left, in came Sayer.

Energetic and fresh-faced, he exuded confidence in the way that only a youthfully fit man in his mid-twenties can. He was tall and well built, his long legs clad in trousers with a faint open check that suggested they were paired with a hand-tailored suit jacket that he had clearly left in his own office. His crisp white shirt had a square-cut Kent collar and a double-button cuff that Agatha knew was the trademark of a certain tailor in London's Jermyn Street. The shirt had never known a tie.

Sayer said good morning, giving Toni an appreciative smile and Agatha a curt nod. He was but a child, she thought, and surely too young for his job, a fact that she could not resist pointing out.

"Human resources manager," she said as he settled into his seat. "That's a big job title. Had we not already met briefly, I should have expected someone a bit more . . . mature."

"I am twenty-eight," Sayer smiled, "and I have a Ph.D. in human resource management. I am not exactly straight out of kindergarten, Mrs. Raisin."

"I'm sorry," said Toni, getting shakily to her feet, clutching her stomach. "I'm afraid I have to go to the, you know . . ."

Agatha nodded and Toni hurried out of the room.

"I do hope she's all right," said Sayer, sounding convincingly concerned.

"Touch of the Delhi belly," said Agatha. "Toni is a glutton for punishment when it comes to wolfing down a vindaloo and a few too many pints."

"Is that so?" said Sayer, raising his eyebrows. "I mean, she looks so slim and —"

"Well, let's get on with it," said Agatha, slightly distracted by the way that every time the young man leaned forward to the table or relaxed back in his chair, muscles beneath the smooth cotton of his shirt moved like kneecaps under a bed sheet. He also had disturbingly red lips. "There are six executives apart from Mr. Morrison. You have some two dozen staff here, but the bulk of them are at your plant in whatsit. Are you responsible for them too?"

"Sekiliv. No, a Sekilivian executive does the hiring and firing there. Different language. Different laws. Different culture. However, he takes his orders from head office."

"So, for whom are you responsible here?"

"The packing and dispatch department, the canteen and cleaners, the security guards, and our resident technician, who fixes everything from leaky pipes to computers."

"I have to say, I was quite surprised that you had employed the circus girl in the packing department. She's very fat."

"Mrs. Raisin! Calling someone fat these days is . . . well, it's like spitting in their face. You can't say things like that."

"Nonetheless," said Agatha with rare patience, "why employ her?"

He had, she thought, rather wet brown eyes, which now took on a faraway look. "It was her circus background, you see." He smiled. "A bit of a boyhood dream. I always fancied the flying trapeze . . . but it's for gymnasts, really, and I," he spread his arms wide, "just grew too big. I wasn't interested in what she looked like. I liked the idea that she'd worked on the trapeze. Anyway, it was only the packing department."

"She is very keen on your canteen. The

little I have eaten there tells me there is a good cook behind the preparation of the meals."

"Yes, old Granny Florence. Mrs. Dinwiddy found her — or rather, she is some sort of family member. I didn't have much to do with her appointment. One does not say no to Mrs. Dinwiddy."

"Why would that be?"

"She is the power behind the throne. Mr. Albert trusts her implicitly. She even has the final say over staff appointments on his behalf."

"That must be rather galling for you," Agatha noted, "having a middle-aged woman, a secretary, telling you your job."

"Not at all," said Sayer. "Mrs. Dinwiddy is a delight to work with. Mr. Albert is a very busy man and the fact that he delegates to Mrs. Dinwiddy means that we can get things done."

"We would like to have a word with your security guards, Bream and . . ."

"Angus Bream and Farley Dunster. Angus does days, Farley nights."

"Both ex-SAS?" Agatha was leafing through the files.

"That's right."

"They always are," she said cynically. "If only half those who claim to have been in the regiment actually did serve, they'd have the world's biggest Christmas party. Did you check them out?"

"Not exactly," Sayer admitted. "I mean, they came with good references and they seemed like decent blokes."

That, thought Agatha, did not sound like the attitude that an efficient and ambitious young HR manager should take.

"As he's on days," she said, "I want to talk to Angus Bream next."

"Actually, you can probably talk to both of them this afternoon," Sayer offered. "There's a party for all the staff up at Mr. Albert's house. It's to welcome Mrs. Morrison home. You and your colleague should come along, if she is feeling up to it."

"I'm sure she will be." Agatha smiled. "Hair of the dog and a big greasy fry-up usually sets her straight."

"Really?" Sayer could not hide a look of bewilderment. "I wouldn't have thought . . . I mean, she looks so —"

"And what about the former receptionist — Josie, I think she was called? Why did she leave?"

"You mean Josie Trent? She wanted to travel, see the world. Can't blame her for that."

At that moment, Toni walked back into

the room and Sayer took it as his cue to leave, sighing and shaking his head after stealing one final glance at her.

"What's up with him?" she asked as the door closed.

"He's concerned about your eating habits," said Agatha.

"Ah." Toni nodded. "Delhi belly?"

"With a few added flourishes. Now, how did you get on?"

"It was a good idea to make up an excuse for a sneaky look around. I wandered the corridors taking a look into storerooms and offices. Most are standing empty. There was no one around. This place is like a ghost ship. Even in the packing and dispatch department, the staff were standing about chatting. There was very little work going on. Nothing is happening here. The trapeze girl was sitting with a couple of others, eating iced buns, and drinking tea. I made myself scarce when I saw one of the security guards prowling the department — Dunster, I think. Doesn't he work nights?"

"They're both here for a homecoming party — Mr. Albert's wife. We're invited."

"What's our next move?"

"Iced buns sound good."

"Great," Toni giggled. "I know the way to Granny Florence's café — out the back way and across the courtyard. Let's go!"

Agatha picked up her handbag and a handy umbrella that had been left in the conference room. It looked like rain outside, and the Dior jacket she was wearing was a mix of wool and silk that really couldn't tolerate the wet. She and Toni walked along a barren corridor, the tap of their heels on the cold linoleum the only sound to be heard.

"You were right," she said as they walked. "The place is dead. It makes the Carsely Ladies' Society meetings look like party central. The whole thing seems like a front for something else. A huge scam masquerading as a thriving business."

"And we've become part of the scam," said Toni. "The detectives hired to make it look like there's something worth stealing — to convince outsiders that there's something here to protect."

"Something more than Granny Florence's iced buns, you mean?" Agatha joked. "But we know that the new battery pack, however much delayed, is not here, and . . . Hold on a moment. Did you hear that?"

It came again. An unmistakable two-tone honk. Agatha was entranced.

"It's a donkey," she said. "I can hear a donkey."

"Sayer told me on our last visit that it's a pet that's kept for the boss's wife," said Toni. "There's a stable block on the far side of the old R&D department, on the way up to the manor house."

"I want to see it," said Agatha, suddenly becoming misty-eyed. "I love donkeys."

"Forget it," Toni moaned. "Sticky buns are more fun than a smelly old donkey any day."

But Agatha could not simply forget it. Donkeys represented a childhood dream that had never been fulfilled. Donkeys belonged in a traditionally British picture-postcard world of seaside holiday rides on the sands and family fun in the sunshine at resorts like Weston-super-Mare and Llandudno, which had always sounded more desirably exotic than Scarborough or Skegness. Sadly, as a child she had never been taken to any of those places, and as an adult, Biarritz had always held more allure than Bognor. Yet Agatha, who had no time for most pets or animals other than her own two cats, simply adored donkeys. She headed for a door that would take them outside in the direction of the stable block.

"Okay," sighed Toni, trotting to catch her up. "Let's go see the donkey. Its name is Wizz-Wazz. You never told me you had a thing about donkeys . . ."

Rounding the corner of the near-derelict R&D building, Agatha could see a path leading up over a sloping meadow towards Albert Morrison's house. The gables were just visible beyond the rise. Closer to hand, the cobbled courtyard of the stable block opened out. It was deserted save for a mud-spattered Land Rover parked at the far end. Only one of the loose boxes was occupied, and they could hear the donkey braying a welcome when it realised that it had visitors. By the entrance to the stable was a bucket full of carrots. Agatha selected the cleanest one and tiptoed across the cobbles, determined not to wedge the delicate heels of her elegant Christian Louboutin pumps in the booby-trap cracks between the stones. Halfway across, she gave up and took off her shoes, handing the umbrella to Toni. Carrot in one hand, Louboutins in the other, she approached the loose box.

When she was close enough — and arm's length seemed close enough — she took a good look over the door at the creature inside. It was very hairy; a kind of reddish-brown hair, with a white patch covering its nose and mouth. White rings highlighted large eyes that were as dark as melted chocolate, and when it blinked, it fluttered the longest, most luxurious eyelashes Agatha had ever seen.

"He's really quite . . . lovely?" she said, taking a step nearer, then wrinkling her nose. "But oh! He has serious issues with personal hygiene."

"The loose box badly needs mucking out," said Toni, peering over the door, "and he is a she — a Jenny. Male donkeys are called Jacks."

Agatha gave her a quizzical look.

"I saw something about them on TV once." Toni shrugged. "Anyway, I thought you were the donkey lover."

"Actually," said Agatha, "this is the first time I have ever met a donkey. Perhaps I'm not quite as fond of them as I thought I would be."

She took a step closer and held out the carrot. Wizz-Wazz bared her teeth and lunged, snatching the carrot just as Toni brought the umbrella down sharply across her nose. The donkey stared at her, as though in disbelief. Agatha did the same.

"Why . . . ?"

"I thought it was attacking."

Wizz-Wazz appeared to be thinking, her jaw moving in a circular motion, crunching the carrot. Then she backed up inside the loose box, paused, and charged forward, butting the door, which to Agatha and Toni's shared horror sprang open. Wizz-Wazz crossed the threshold and glowered at Toni, her brown eyes narrowing to sinister slits and turning a disturbingly evil red. Agatha bravely took a sideways step, arms outstretched, one Louboutin stiletto in each hand, putting herself between Toni and the donkey. She immediately wondered why. Wasn't it Toni who had got them into this mess? Making any other sudden moves, however, now seemed unwise.

Wizz-Wazz took a few more moments to decide how she felt about being whacked with an umbrella, then finally made up her mind. If ever a donkey was filled with anger, Wizz-Wazz was. Her teeth appeared once more, and she thrust her head forward and let out a roaring bray, spraying Agatha with a shower of spit and chewed carrot.

As the beast took a deep breath, preparing a second volley, Agatha could think of only one thing to do.

"RUN!!!"

The two women sprinted as fast as their legs could carry them, pausing only to catch their breath when they reached the corner of the R&D building. Out of sight of the stables, they leant against the wall, breathing heavily.

"I don't think," gasped Agatha, surveying her spit-and-carrot-spattered clothes, "that I have ever been —"

"Not now, Agatha!" yelled Toni, squinting round the corner. "She's coming after us!"

They took off towards the main building, slamming into the door they had used previously only to find there was no handle on the outside. It was a fire door, and could be opened only from the inside. Wizz-Wazz popped her head round the corner of R&D and glared at them, showing them her fearsome yellow teeth. The top set moved to the left, the bottom set to the right, as though they had minds of their own, and Wizz-Wazz let out a hideous hiss.

"The car park!" Toni yelled. "It's our only chance!"

Dashing to where they had parked by the main entrance to the building, they flopped into the car and Toni fired up the engine, spinning the wheels as she raced for the factory gates.

"I blame you for this," Agatha puffed, struggling to catch her breath as she picked gloopy carrot out of her hair and clawed at the orange gunge on her jacket.

"I wasn't the one who wanted to see the wretched donkey," Toni said, defending herself.

"No, but you were the one who battered it with your brolly like some demented gladiator! Why did you do that?"

"I was trying to save you — it was communicating hostility and aggression."

"Well, thank you, Dr. Dolittle! It might simply have wanted the carrot."

"It might simply have bitten your fingers off!"

"Oh, what are a few fingers compared with a once-in-a-lifetime jacket like this?" Agatha wailed, swiping at the spreading orange stains. "Take me home. I need to get changed. We will talk about this later."

They drove in silence through the centre of Mircester to pick up the Carsely road, the mood in the car as heavy as the dark storm clouds gathering overhead.

CHAPTER THREE

Agatha showered, washed the gloop out of her hair, and carefully reapplied her make-up. Rummaging in her wardrobe, she chose a white silk top with a plunging neckline, pairing it with a dusky pink Ted Baker jacket. The tailoring of the jacket flattered her figure whether it was buttoned or left open. She decided to leave it open. The matching trousers finished mid-calf. Coupled with high-heeled grey sandals, the trousers had the effect of making her legs look longer. Pink, thought Agatha, glancing out of her bedroom window at the leaden sky. Too summery? Well, they were going to a party after all, and she would be in competition with Toni, who had emerged unscathed from the carrot fallout, and Mrs. Morrison, who was, according to Sayer, a woman of remarkable beauty.

Taking one final look in the full-length mirror, Agatha sighed. Could she compete?

Should she even try? And compete for what? It wasn't as if there was any man at the factory she would remotely consider setting her sights on. The muscular Mr. Sayer was intriguing but had barely outgrown his spots. So what was so intriguing about him really? Something odd. Something that wasn't right. On the other hand, that pretty much summed up everyone she had met at Morrison's.

She looked at the sad face staring back at her from the mirror and gave herself a mental shake. Snap out of it, Agatha! You do not have to compete with other women. You are Agatha Raisin and *they* have to compete with *you*! She grabbed a favourite jacket from the back of a chair. The deep red fun fur was frivolous and youthful, but why the hell should the young have all the fun?

Downstairs in her living room, she found Toni sending a text message on her phone.

"Boyfriend?" she asked.

"No . . . I mean, well . . ." stammered Toni.

"Never mind that now," said Agatha. "This morning with that donkey. I've decided that we shall say no more about it." She then proceeded to say a great deal more about it, ending a monologue of several minutes with ". . . so rash decisions can have dire consequences and . . . What on earth is the matter?"

Toni's chest heaved as she fought back a sob. What's got into her? wondered Agatha. I hardly said a thing.

"It's just that . . ." Toni passed her phone from one hand to the other.

"Man trouble," said Agatha. She had delivered her lecture standing by the fireplace but now sat down on the sofa beside Toni, perching near the edge of the cushion so as not to crease her trousers. Agatha was not known for her forgiving nature, mainly because she didn't have one. Neither was she prone to spontaneous outbursts of sympathy, but if they were to find out what was going on at Morrison's, she needed her assistant to be on top form, not blubbing like a lovesick teenager. Then it struck her that, actually, Toni really was little more than a teenager. "You . . . um . . . want to talk about it?"

She felt she should put her arm around the girl, then saw a huge tear leave a trail of mascara down Toni's cheek and decided against it. Having one jacket ruined in a day was quite enough. She reached for a box of tissues and handed her those instead.

"It's just that . . ." Toni said in a near

whisper, "he really wants to get married . . . and I do too, but —"

"But not to him," Agatha cut in helpfully. "You're not actually in love with him, are you?"

"I don't know," said Toni.

"Then you're not," Agatha proclaimed. "You would know if you were, and any marriage that does not start out with the newlyweds totally in love is doomed."

"I kind of knew you would say that."

"Then you know that I am right," said Agatha. "I am always right."

"But I think he's in love with me."

"Of course he is," Agatha assured her. "Why wouldn't he be? You are gorgeous. You are every young man's dream. Pretty much every old man's too. Not right now, though. Right now, you look frightful." Then she smiled and added, "But even your frightful looks pretty damn good."

"I'd better sort myself out," said Toni, blowing her nose with a honk so loud that it would have made even Wizz-Wazz proud.

"You know where the bathroom is," said Agatha. "Hurry up. We have a party to go to, and I could do with a drink."

"Ah . . ." said Toni, pausing at the living room door. "I spoke to Mrs. Dinwiddy while you were getting ready, to find out

71

what would be happening this afternoon. The only drink served at Mrs. Morrison's homecoming party will be tea."

"What?" said Agatha. "What kind of a welcome home is that? Doesn't she like a drink?"

"A bit too much," Toni replied, climbing the stairs. "Mrs. Morrison is coming home from a spell in a rather exclusive and expensive rehab clinic."

Agatha crossed the room, opened the doors of her cabinet and poured herself a gin and tonic.

As Toni drove her to Albert Morrison's house, Agatha ran through the events of the morning in her head, up to the part where they had encountered Wizz-Wazz. That incident, she decided, needed to be parked way at the back of her mind. One day in the dim and distant future, she might be able to laugh about it. On the other hand, maybe not.

"Something is bothering me about John Sayer," she said. "He seemed very sure of himself. Quite cocky."

"I've read through his personnel file," said Toni. "There was nothing much in it. It mentioned some public school that I'd never heard of, his degree from a minor university, then nothing until he started at Morrison's about a year ago. He doesn't earn a huge salary."

"That's it," said Agatha. "That's the strange thing. He's not paid a great deal, yet he clearly spends a fortune on his clothes. Where does he get the money?"

The only other man she knew who had such expensive taste in clothes was Charles. Granted, his estate generated very little income, certainly not enough to maintain the house and his extravagant lifestyle, but Agatha had helped him to straighten out his finances by putting him in touch with the best broker in the City, the man who looked after her own investments. That had worked well enough to keep him in the black ever since, although he was never going to be rolling in cash. "Land rich and cash poor" was the phrase that popped into Agatha's head. That would not, she pondered, ever be the case with young Mr. Sayer. He was not one of the elite, a member of the English upper class, and without the right family background he never would be, no matter how many years he spent trying to dress the part.

How many years? That, she suddenly re-alised, was the other problem with Sayer.

"So he went to university," she recapped,

"and started with Morrison's a year ago."

"That's right," said Toni. "No other jobs on file."

"But he would have left university when he was around twenty-one," said Agatha, "and started at Morrison's when he was twenty-seven. Where the hell was he for those six years?"

"Good point," Toni agreed. "Something else that I found odd. Remember how flustered Mrs. Dinwiddy was yesterday evening? She desperately wanted us out before the security guard came round. It was almost as if she were frightened of him."

"Good point from you," said Agatha. "Let's try to get her on her own again. If we put her on the spot, maybe she'll let something slip."

Toni turned left through two tall stone gateposts topped with giant stone pineapples.

"Pineapples?" she said. "What's that all about?"

"A sign of wealth," explained Agatha, recalling something Charles had once told her when they were tucking into a dessert of pineapple upside-down cake to round off a lavish dinner at the Savoy. (She had paid.) "When this house was built in the eighteenth century, only the super-rich could afford the expense of growing pineapples in hothouses or importing them from abroad. They would use one as a dinner table centrepiece. It wasn't for eating, just a decoration — for showing off. They used it again and again until it started to rot."

They cruised past the stable block, home to the fearsome Wizz-Wazz, the driveway taking a far shorter route to the house than the winding path from the factory. Beyond a pair of majestic oak trees, the front of the house came into view, the yellow stone topped with a slate roof. There were three white-framed windows either side of the ornate front doorway. A matching set of windows identified the upper floor, and in the roof were a couple of triangular dormers. The old servants' quarters, no doubt, thought Agatha, admiring the building. It was nowhere near as big as Charles's rambling pile; large enough to impress, yet small enough for comfortable living.

Toni parked alongside several other cars to the left of the house. As she and Agatha walked towards the heavy oak front door, it was opened by Angus Bream, who had clearly seen them arrive. He nodded a curt greeting and they stepped into a large reception hall. At one end was an ornate fireplace, although no fire was burning in the grate. A series of polished wooden doors led off the hall, and at the other end was a wide staircase, sweeping up to the left. Morrison's staff, most of whom Agatha had never seen before, were standing around in groups of three or four, balancing a teacup on a saucer in one hand, the other plucking dainty morsels from serving trays that were being passed around by black-clad waitresses.

They had arrived just in time. John Sayer, standing by the fireplace and now wearing a jacket that Agatha deemed a little too tight across the biceps, but still no tie, held aloft a small silver bell and gave it a tinkle. Conversation in the room subsided to a murmur and then died completely as Mr. Albert Morrison stepped forward. In the few days since they had last met, thought Agatha, Mr. Albert had managed to grow even more insipid. What hair he still had was a mousy brown colour and combed back in thinning strands over his gleaming white scalp. His stocky build was made to look positively rotund in the presence of Sayer, hovering at his shoulder, and the wiry Farley Dunster, who had stationed himself a little further back.

Morrison removed his horn-rimmed spectacles, folded them carefully and tucked them into the breast pocket of his dark blue blazer.

"Good afternoon, everyone," he said, "and welcome to our home. As you know, we have always regarded Morrison's as a family business, and all of you are part of that family."

"I haven't heard anyone sound so insincere," Agatha whispered in Toni's ear, "since that salesman sold you your crappy little car."

"Shh!!" A small man in front of them turned and hissed. Agatha curled her top lip at him and he quickly looked away.

"That is why," Morrison continued, "we have invited you all here once again to welcome home my lovely wife, Mrs. Aphrodite Morrison." He waved an arm towards the staircase, and Agatha just had time to register that "once again" surely meant that this was not the first time Aphrodite had checked in to dry out before she turned to behold a vision on the stairs.

Aphrodite was truly beautiful. She was tall and slim and posed with one hand on the banister and the other hanging elegantly by her side. Her slender arm was, thought Agatha, almost certainly weighed down by the size of the diamond on her finger, which was shooting light beams across the room.

Less of a ring, more of a glitter ball. Agatha reached out her hand, put a finger on Toni's chin and closed her mouth.

With her long white sleeveless gown shimmering as only the finest silk can, Aphrodite made her way down the stairs, her family of employees applauding every step. The gown was gathered at the waist by a garland of myrtle leaves and rosebuds — the flowers of the Greek goddess Aphrodite, Agatha recalled from a Greek-themed fashion shoot when she was in PR what seemed like a lifetime ago. She marvelled at Aphrodite's hair. It was golden blonde, held in high waves by a jewelled Alice band that stopped only a little short of tiara status, yet it still managed to cascade in ringlets down to her shoulders. Not all of that could be real, she decided. Extensions, surely. No one had *that* much hair.

The crowd parted as Aphrodite crossed the floor to take her husband's outstretched hand. She was at least twenty years younger than Albert, whom Agatha reckoned was probably around fifty. She smiled and nodded to people as she glided past. Smiling without a trace of a wrinkle on that perfect skin, Agatha noted. Then suddenly the smile vanished, Aphrodite's eyes narrowed and her expression turned from gracious delight to absolute fury in the blink of an eye.

"Where in hell's name has yous put my Wizz-Wazz?" shrieked the goddess.

"Darling, this is hardly the place for a donkey," her husband calmly explained. "We can't have her in the house."

"It's my goddamned party and I wanna see my Wizz-Wazz!" Aphrodite howled in a voice that was somewhere between a police siren and a ruptured bagpipe.

"Don't worry, darling," Morrison consoled his wife. "We will have Wizz-Wazz here in just a tick."

Agatha, who had sidled closer for a better view of proceedings, now observed another transformation as Albert Morrison turned to John Sayer and went from mild-mannered factory owner to sinister bully.

"Dinwiddy is still at the factory," he snapped. "Tell her to go to the stables and get Peter to bring the donkey up here."

He looked round, saw Agatha listening and fixed her with a venomous stare. Agatha backed away and grabbed Toni by the arm. Mrs. Morrison had fallen silent, eerily restored to beauty.

"What sort of accent would you say she had?" Toni asked.

"Sounded like rural Gloucester overlaid with Brooklyn slum and screech owl," Agatha replied. "Come on. Drive me down to the stables. This could be our chance to catch Dinwiddy off guard."

Taking the short route to the stables down the main drive, Agatha and Toni were there in moments. A chill wind was beginning to blow as they left the car, and Agatha pulled the fun fur tighter as she walked round to the stable block entrance.

"Morrison said Mrs. Dinwiddy was still at the factory," she told Toni. "I'll check here and you check the factory. Let's see if we can find her."

But as she turned into the stable courtyard, she stopped short.

"Toni!" she yelled. "Come back! I've found her . . ."

Mrs. Dinwiddy lay on the cobbles. Blood was oozing from a vicious wound at the back of her head. Her mouth gaped open and her eyes stared sightlessly. Beside her stood Wizz-Wazz, silent and motionless.

Toni appeared at Agatha's side and took in the scene. Rushing past, she knelt beside Mrs. Dinwiddy and felt for a pulse.

"We . . . we should call an ambulance," said Agatha, fumbling for her phone, although she knew in her heart what her assistant was about to tell her.

"Too late for that," said Toni, "Mrs.

Dinwiddy is dead."

Agatha walked over to where Wizz-Wazz stood gazing at the body, her huge dark eyes focused solely on the patch of cobbles where Mrs. Dinwiddy lay. Toni was already on her phone, talking to the police. Agatha laid her hand on the donkey's back. The hair felt coarse and spiky, and the animal's hide shivered under her touch. Wizz-Wazz was trembling, and now that Agatha was closer, she could hear a quiet low moaning emanating from deep within the donkey.

"You poor girl," she whispered gently. "You're terrified, aren't you? I think you know how this happened."

She slipped off the fun fur and draped it over Wizz-Wazz's back to comfort her, tying the arms loosely around the donkey's neck. What on earth am I doing? she thought. I love that coat. It's far too good for a smelly old . . . But the sight of Wizz-Wazz staring at the corpse made her heart miss a beat. She stroked the creature's nose, then suddenly wondered if Wizz-Wazz might also be injured. She looked down. To her horror, she saw that the donkey's rear hooves were coated with blood, and a neat pattern of dark red splash marks covered her hind legs. It was glaringly obvious that this was not the donkey's own blood.

"No!" she gasped, taking a step back. "You couldn't have . . ."

By the time the police arrived, a small crowd of Morrison's employees had gathered. There was no sign of either Albert or Aphrodite, but the security guards, Bream and Dunster, had sensibly held everyone back from the stable yard, which, apart from Mrs. Dinwiddy's body and the traumatised Wizz-Wazz, was completely empty. The donkey had not moved an inch. Agatha stood near the entrance to the cobbled yard, smoking a cigarette. John Sayer directed the first police officers and an ambulance crew to the body.

Agatha could see Toni sitting in her car, talking on her phone. The boyfriend again, no doubt. She wondered what he looked like. He must be handsome. Toni would surely never land herself with anyone who wasn't at least good-looking. Agatha herself never had. Some of her past lovers had been wealthy, some not so wealthy — Charles certainly fell into that category — but none had been ugly. She would never want to be seen on the arm of a man whom other women did not find attractive. That was the whole point of men. You could show them off like new shoes or a suntan in January when everyone else was looking pale and dreary.

Men could, she conceded, also be good company from time to time. Charles was definitely good company. She wondered where he was, what he was doing. Not standing about in a draughty stable yard catching a chill, that was for sure. Oh, what am I doing here? she thought. How did I get myself into this mess? What am I doing blundering about in a boring battery plant with a manic donkey and now a dead secretary?

Just then another couple of police cars rolled up. Bill Wong emerged from the first one and walked over to Agatha.

"Are you okay?" he asked.

"That tie is shocking," said Agatha, pointing at the offending item around Bill's neck. "Doesn't go with your suit. Doesn't go with your colouring. Not in your swatch at all."

"But . . . but Alice bought it for me."

"Don't let her dress you, Bill. You need a girl who wants to *un*dress you, not the other way round."

"Let's not go there, Agatha," sighed Bill. "Now, can you fill me in on what's happened here?"

Agatha explained about the party, Aphrodite, Wizz-Wazz and the run-in she and Toni had previously had with the donkey. As she spoke, the lanky figure of Chief Inspector Wilkes appeared, along with a shorter man she recognised as the pathologist, Dr Charles Bunbury. While Bunbury proceeded to examine the body, Wilkes rounded on Agatha.

"A real body this time," he grunted. "Not just a leg. Not just a fake leg. A real body. You must be very pleased with yourself, Mrs. Raisin."

"Pleased?" said Agatha. "How could you possibly think anyone could be pleased to find . . . *that*?"

"I understand you were first on the scene of the accident," said Wilkes. "I hope you didn't —"

"It's a bit premature to write this off as an accident, isn't it?" Agatha interrupted him.

"Preliminary reports from my officers indicate precisely that," said Wilkes, "and I expect the coroner will confirm it. What I don't need is a bumbling amateur like yourself sticking her nose in where it's not wanted."

"Bumbling?" cried Agatha. "I think, Inspector, that my record from previous investigations shows —"

"You will leave any investigating that is required to my officers!" barked Wilkes.

"And it's *Chief* Inspector!"

"Really?" said Agatha. "And what do you have to do to become a *chief* inspector nowadays? Send off half a dozen bottle tops and supply a snappy slogan about crime prevention?"

"Make sure you get a complete statement from this witness, Sergeant," Wilkes ordered, turning on his heel to join Dr. Bunbury by the body of Mrs. Dinwiddy.

"Agatha," said Bill once Wilkes was far enough away. "You can't speak to him like that. He is my boss."

"Poor you," said Agatha, taking a couple of steps closer to where Dr. Bunbury was kneeling beside the body. "Quiet now. I want to hear what the pathologist has to say."

"There doesn't appear to be much doubt about the cause of death," Bunbury pronounced, rising to his feet and stripping off a pair of bloodied latex gloves. "Blunt-force trauma to the back of the head, although I will be able to confirm that after the postmortem. And it looks like you already have the culprit in custody. The shape of the wound is consistent with the victim having been kicked by a hoof. This is the likely killer," he added, nodding towards Wizz-Wazz. "Caught red-handed, or rather, red-hoofed."

"As I thought," crowed Wilkes triumphantly, turning towards Agatha. "Clearly an accident."

"But . . . but look at her shoes," said Agatha. "Don't you think it even a little strange that we find a leg wearing Mrs. Dinwiddy's shoe, and just a couple of days later this happens?"

"I think it is tragic, Mrs. Raisin. That's what I think. A tragic accident, that's what this is, and I don't want you blundering around trying to prove anything different!"

"The real tragedy is that you're in charge," said Agatha. "I don't think you could spot a crime if it jumped out of your lunch and mugged you."

"I really couldn't care less what you think," said Wilkes, rounding on Bill. "I want this all cleared up with the minimum of fuss, Sergeant. Not a second more of police time is to be spent on it than is absolutely necessary. We have enough on our plate as it is."

Wilkes stormed off to his car, and Bill left Agatha alone for a few moments while he spoke to his uniformed colleagues.

"What will happen to Wizz-Wazz?" asked Agatha, catching up with him again.

"I can't say," said Bill, sounding, Agatha

thought, more than a little annoyed with her. "The vet has checked the donkey and it is uninjured. It's really none of your concern, Agatha."

At that moment, a swarthy little man wearing a flat cap and a muddy waxed jacket came shambling up to them. His hands were crammed into the jacket pockets, and he had a copy of the *Racing Post* folded under one arm and a cigarette hanging from his mouth.

"What's goin' on here, then?" he said.

"Who are you?" asked Bill.

"Peter Trotter," answered the man, pointing to a first-floor window. "That's my flat above the stables. I look after that there donkey for Mrs. Morrison. Is that the Dinwiddy woman lyin' there?"

"Where have you been?" said Bill.

"Down the betting shop in Mircester. Had a tip on the four thirty at Cheltenham."

"Don't go anywhere," ordered Bill. "One of these officers will need to take a statement from you. In the meantime, maybe you could move the donkey into its loose box. Forensics and the vet are finished with it."

Stuffing the newspaper into his pocket, Trotter collected a halter that was hanging on the wall, then walked over to Wizz-Wazz.

Having fitted the halter over her head, he tightened it up and gave the attached leading rein a tug.

"Come on, you miserable old bitch," he coughed.

Wizz-Wazz refused to budge.

"Move it!" yelled Trotter. "I ain't got all night!"

Still the donkey stubbornly stood her ground. Trotter grabbed the *Racing Post* from his pocket, rolled it into a baton and smacked her on the side of the head.

"What do you think you're doing?" screamed Agatha, charging over to confront him. "Can't you see she's upset?"

"Mind your own business, you stupid tart!" spat Trotter.

Agatha tensed. She tilted her head ever so slightly to one side. "What," she growled, "did you just say?"

"I said —" But Trotter never had the chance to repeat himself. Agatha snatched the newspaper from his hand and walloped him right and left across the face.

"Stop that!" called Bill Wong, stepping between them and catching hold of her wrist before she could deliver another flurry of blows. "What are you playing at, Agatha?"

"You saw what he just did!" said Agatha.

"An' you saw what *she* just did," snarled Trotter, pointing a grubby finger at her. "That were assault. Well, I ain't gonna press charges, Officer, but I ain't gonna forget, neither."

Agatha turned her back on him and picked up the leading rein. "Come along, Wizz-Wazz," she said, and the donkey, calm and compliant, followed her to the loose box.

"Agatha," said Bill. "Go home now. We'll talk about all of this again tomorrow."

It had started to rain by the time Agatha and Toni were heading down the driveway towards the pineapple gates. Agatha fidgeted with her handbag. She wanted to smoke but did not want to roll down the window for fear of letting in the rain.

Toni turned right onto the road towards Mircester. "I suppose it could have been an accident," she said, peering through the windscreen, where the wipers had smeared bug splats across her line of sight. "I mean, we know that Wizz-Wazz can be really aggressive."

"Calling that an accident is like saying that the taps on my kitchen sink pour neat gin," said Agatha. "It would be very convenient, but there's not a shred of truth in it. There are just too many fishy things going on around Morrison's. And there was definitely something wrong about that scene in the stable yard."

She pictured the cobbled yard in her mind, trying to visualise what it was that was nagging at her, the thing that was dancing up and down at the back of her mind yelling "Look at me! I'm here! I'm obvious, you stupid tart!" That made her think of Trotter, and that, in turn, made her picture Wizz-Wazz.

"Oh bugger," she groaned. "I left my beautiful coat draped around that bloody animal's neck!"

"Do you want to go back for it?" asked Toni, slowing the car.

"No, it can wait," Agatha replied, "and it will give me an excuse to revisit the stables tomorrow. I need to find out what really happened there. That was no accident, Toni. Mrs. Dinwiddy was murdered."

"It did look like the donkey lashed out and killed her, Agatha," said Toni.

"I think that is what it was meant to look like," Agatha countered. "And the police and everyone else have fallen for it."

"But how can you make a donkey kill someone?" asked Toni. "Death by donkey — it's not something I've ever heard of before."

"Wizz-Wazz didn't kill that woman," said Agatha. "I'm no great animal lover, but I could feel how terrified she was. And the blood spatters up the back of her legs didn't look right. They were too neat, too regular, too perfect. There was nothing random about them. It was as if they had been painted on. It was murder all right. I don't yet know how it was done, but I intend to find out."

"It's certainly strange," said Toni, turning off the A44 onto the familiar road down into Carsely. "Strange that this should happen now, when we know that something dodgy is going on at the factory."

"Strange is not the word for it," Agatha said. "Suspicious is what I would call it. I smell a rat — a murdering rat."

"A murdering rat that's framed a donkey," said Toni.

"I get the feeling you're not taking this seriously," Agatha scolded.

The headlights swept across the rain-battered lilac trees that led to Agatha's cottage. Toni pulled up at the garden gate.

"Right," said Agatha. "I'll see you at the office bright and early tomorrow. By then I will have figured out what we should do next."

"I will be a little late tomorrow, remember?" said Toni. "I mentioned that I had a dental appointment."

"Right," Agatha sighed. "Well, let's talk tomorrow once you're finished in the torture chair."

"It's just a routine check." Toni smiled. "Will you be okay this evening on your own? I mean, I could stay with you if you . . ."

"No, I'll be fine," said Agatha. "I'm sure you have somewhere else you would rather be."

"Well, I . . ."

"See you tomorrow, then."

Agatha hurried up the short garden path, shoulders hunched and head down against the rain. She fumbled with her keys and then darted inside, shaking rain out of her hair as she flipped the light switch. Boswell and Hodge came trotting down the hall towards her, tails up and eyes bright.

"Hello, you two," she cooed. "This is a lovely welcome. I guess you're both hungry, aren't you?" She stooped to stroke the cats as they wound themselves around her legs, swaying in and out of her ankles. "Let's go through to the kitchen and get you some food." They felt soft and warm, comforting, pleasing to touch. Their fur was so much more sleek and smooth than the coarse hair on Wizz-Wazz's back. And they were purring loudly, the rhythmic rumble throbbing like tiny engines somewhere in their chests. Agatha stroked their heads and tickled their backs. These were real pets. What kind of nutcase kept a psycho donkey — an animal that sprayed you with carrot spit and then made you run for your life?

She couldn't imagine Aphrodite Morrison taking any real interest in Wizz-Wazz. How could the donkey ever play any part in that woman's lifestyle? She didn't seem to fit in. She was just too headstrong, too independent, too demanding, too unpredictable, too smelly. Maybe, thought Agatha, I'm a bit like Wizz-Wazz. Apart from the smelly bit, obviously. Maybe neither of us really fit in. Maybe we are both condemned to be lonely.

She wondered how she had ended up on her own tonight. James was off drooling over some dusty monument up a mountain no one had ever heard of in a country no one could care less about, but where was Charles? He, or more likely Gustav, must have heard on the grapevine by now that she had another tricky situation on her hands. Charles had told her he was interested in the Morrison's affair, so where was he now that the case, which had been merely interesting, had turned to murder?

But was it really murder? Agatha filled the

cats' bowls with food and considered the gruesome fate of poor Mrs. Dinwiddy. She had been an irritating, irksome woman, but who would really want her dead?

In the unlikely event that she had been having an affair with Albert Morrison and things had turned nasty, it was feasible that either he or Aphrodite might want rid of her. She had worked closely with John Sayer. Maybe she had discovered something about his mysterious past that had cost her her life. And what about Josie, the former receptionist, who might have been a rival for Albert Morrison's affections? Could she be mixed up in it? Or maybe it was something to do with the security guard about whom Dinwiddy seemed so nervous.

Agatha sighed. Watching the cats devour their food made her realise that she hadn't eaten properly all day. She opened the freezer and fished out a couple of ready meals that could be nuked in the microwave straight from frozen. Chicken curry or lasagne, which was it to be? Neither. She shoved them both back in their frosty graves, lit a cigarette, and poured herself a glass of wine.

She replayed the discovery of the body in her mind, pausing at the shoes Dinwiddy was wearing. Brogues, just like the one on the fake leg. Only these were on feet attached to real legs, attached to the unfortunate Mrs. Dinwiddy. If she had been murdered, then how was it done? No one could use a donkey as a murder weapon, could they? No, Agatha was convinced that Wizz-Wazz was not the killer. Those blood spatter marks were simply too pristine. Someone was trying to make a murder look like an accident. So who had killed Mrs. Dinwiddy, and how, and why?

She heard a light knock at her front door. Who could that be? Charles? He was here at last! She opened the door to find Margaret Bloxby, the vicar's wife, standing there wearing oven gloves and holding a casserole dish.

"I heard that something ghastly happened at Morrison's," said Mrs. Bloxby. "You must have had a terrible shock. I thought you could use some company."

"You are indeed a sight for sore eyes," said Agatha. "Come in out of the rain."

Mrs. Bloxby headed straight for the kitchen, saying, "And I bet you haven't eaten today, so I made a casserole. Alf is busy working on one of his sermons; he won't miss me. I thought I might stay in your spare room so that you're not alone."

"Thank you," said Agatha, suddenly feeling exhausted and with tears welling in her eyes. "You are a true friend."

"Now," said Mrs. Bloxby, laying a couple of plates on the table. "Tell me all about it."

CHAPTER FOUR

Agatha sat across the breakfast table from Mrs. Bloxby, drinking coffee and nibbling freshly buttered toast. She had woken to the smell of the toast, thrown on her dressing gown and dashed downstairs to find the vicar's wife preparing a light breakfast.

"You look much better this morning," said Mrs. Bloxby. "It's amazing what a good night's rest can do for you."

"That's thanks to you," said Agatha. "Your casserole was delicious, and offloading onto you about Morrison's and the murder was just what I needed to help get it all straight in my mind."

"Well, I'm always around if you need me," smiled Mrs. Bloxby, "and from what you told me, it sounds as if that poor woman definitely was murdered. But you mustn't try to solve the case all on your own. Toni will help, and you need to use your man Patrick Mulligan, too."

"I will," agreed Agatha, wiping crumbs from her mouth. "He must need a break from that hotel job. He can use his contacts to do background checks on some of these people, starting with the security guards and John Sayer. I'll get Toni to join me up at the factory later. I want to know what people there think about this, and I want to have another snoop around."

"I'd best be off, then," said Mrs. Bloxby, shrugging on her coat. "I have a Carsely Ladies' Society committee meeting at ten, and the Mircester Choristers are rehearsing in the church hall at noon. That should be different. The conductor has an interesting idea about combining Monteverdi with Motörhead. I suppose Alf will be wanting some breakfast, too."

"Thanks again for last night!" Agatha called breezily as Mrs. Bloxby made for the door. "I'd best get myself ready. Raisin Investigations is on the trail of a murderer!"

Toni sat in the dentist's waiting room. She always tried to be punctual for appointments with the doctor or the dentist, but they rarely saw her on time. She was always left waiting. She had been waiting for more than ten minutes and it was becoming tedious.

She gazed at the posters on the walls. One showed a revolting photograph of a man with his mouth propped open, displaying broken, blackened, and rotting teeth with dark gaps between them. His gums were red and inflamed and the whole thing really didn't look much like a human mouth at all. It had the appearance of a wounded sea creature or some kind of alien just landed from the planet Stinky Decay. A second photograph showed the man smiling, having had all of the bad teeth removed and replaced with gleaming new dental implants. It was supposed to demonstrate how the implants changed the man's looks, and presumably his life, completely. In fact, it looked like exactly the same man wearing someone else's teeth. He looked like a tooth burglar. Toni thought tooth theft would be a crime worthy of investigation by the great Chief Inspector Wilkes . . . or maybe he would find a way to write that off as an accident, too.

The next poster showed a young couple strolling hand in hand along a deserted beach under a clear blue sky, their dazzling smiles outshining the sun. It was an advertisement for tooth whitening. Toni wondered if the couple were really as much in love as they looked. She didn't think so. After all, they were only models, weren't they? They weren't real people. They could pretend to be in love for as long as it took to get that one photograph for the poster. They didn't have to spend any time together. They didn't have to spend the rest of their lives together or meet each other's families. They didn't have to pretend to like the same music, the same TV shows or the same colour of paint for the living room walls. They might not even like each other. They probably made catty comments about each other to the photographer. She'd say he spent more time fussing with his hair and applying his anti-wrinkle cream than she did. He'd say she could do with shaving her legs more often, and her top lip while she was at it. Maybe the only thing the poster couple had in common was unfeasibly white teeth.

Toni sighed. She was trying desperately hard to fight off the thought that she and her young doctor had very little in common. Perhaps he was simply not the right man for her. Or perhaps he was the right man, just at the wrong time. Perhaps she was not yet ready for the relationship she thought she wanted. How could she explain that to him? She tutted with frustration and snatched a society magazine from a pile on the chair next to her. To her surprise, it was an issue from this year. In fact, it was from this month, published just a few days ago.

She flicked through pages packed with advertisements for clothes, jewellery, watches, cars, and houses that she would never be able to afford. She scanned one photograph after another of aristocrats and minor royals leaving nightclubs and restaurants that she would also never be able to afford. Then she stopped and thumbed back a couple of pages. She was sure she had seen a face she recognised. Yes, there it was — Charles. He was looking particularly dapper in an evening suit with black tie, and on his arm was a painfully plain-looking young woman.

Sir Charles Fraith, the picture caption announced, *leaving a family dinner at the Savoy with Miss Mary Darlinda Brown-Field. The dinner marked a special celebration. Miss Brown-Field said . . .*

" '. . . I am delighted to announce my engagement to Charles'!" gasped Toni, reading aloud.

"That's nice, dear," smiled an old lady sitting in the corner.

"No, not me," Toni started to explain. "It's my . . . Oh, never mind."

"Miss Toni Gilmour?" A dental nurse

poked her head round the waiting room door.

"Not for long," chirped the old lady. "She's just got engaged, you know."

"Really?" said the nurse. "Congratulations, Miss Gilmour."

"No, no, it's not me," said Toni, dropping the magazine back on the pile as she stood up. It's never going to be me, she thought as she followed the nurse into the surgery. She might have allowed a dark cloak of depression to weigh her down at that thought had it not been for the sudden dread she felt when she realised that Agatha knew nothing about Sir Charles's engagement. She was going to go batshit crazy! Toni knew she would have to tell her eventually, but prayed that Sir Charles would pluck up the courage to do so first. She did not want to be anywhere in the vicinity when that particular tornado touched down. The dubious delights of the dentist's chair were far preferable to being caught up in the wake of Agatha Raisin on the rampage.

Agatha had just finished dressing when she heard a knock at the door. She had chosen a black crêpe Valentino dress with embroidered macramé blossom inlaid on the sleeves. That seemed the right sort of thing to wear given that she was visiting a place where one of the employees had been killed — murdered — the previous day. Then she relented. Black was fine for mourning, but not for morning. She picked out a red Preen dress instead, showing her respect for the deceased Mrs. Dinwiddy by pairing it with a black handbag and black suede boots. The soles of the boots were a bit too slippery and the heels a little too high for her to rush downstairs to answer the door, so she picked her way down sideways. There was a second drum of knocks.

"Hold on, I'm coming!" she yelled to whoever was outside. Toni? No, she was at the dentist. Bill Wong? Probably. He'd said he would talk to her today. "I'm just taking it easy on the stairs." Reaching the floor, she took two confident strides forward to open the door. "But I'm much better on . . . Charles!"

Sir Charles Fraith stood on the doorstep, immaculate as always. The only thing about him that looked even slightly askew was his marginally crooked, unusually awkward smile.

"Morning, Aggie," he said. "I heard you had a spot of bother and —"

"Where the hell have you been, then?" said Agatha. "I thought you might have come round yesterday evening."

"I would have," said Charles, "but there was something else I had to attend to. I've been meaning to have a word with you about —"

"Well, it will have to wait," Agatha replied, grabbing a raincoat and waving him away from the door. "But now you are here, you can drive me to Morrison's. I have to make a few phone calls and I can fill you in on the way. You said you were interested in this case, so now's the time to start showing it. Let's go."

When they arrived at Morrison's, the factory gates were closed and Farley Dunster emerged from the gatehouse. He stooped to look into the car as Charles wound down the window. Dunster had a hard, lean face with thin lips.

"Mrs. Raisin," he said. "I didn't recognise the car." He looked towards Charles. "And you are, sir?"

"He is one of my associates," Agatha explained. "I need his help to finish going through the personnel files and talking to the staff."

"No one here today, Mrs. Raisin," said Dunster. "They've all been given the day off on account of what happened yesterday."

"Not you, though, Mr. Dunster? And I

thought you worked nights."

"Normally do, but Angus is inside on the reception desk, fielding calls and suchlike. If you want to sort through those files, I'll let him know you're coming."

Dunster returned to the gatehouse and picked up the phone, speaking for only a few moments before pressing a button on his desk to open the gates. By the time Agatha and Charles pulled up outside the entrance to the factory, Angus Bream was there waiting for them.

"Didn't expect to see you here today, Mrs. Raisin," said Bream. "The place is deserted."

"No rest for the wicked." Agatha smiled at him. "We have a contract with Morrison's and I need to get back to work."

"All your files are still in the conference room," said Bream. "I'll show you upstairs."

"That's all right. I know the way," Agatha told him, stepping forward.

"Nevertheless," Bream insisted, moving in front of her, "I will show you up there."

Upstairs, he opened the conference room door, then left Agatha and Charles alone.

"I get the impression," said Charles, "that we were just escorted onto the premises."

"Undoubtedly." Agatha nodded. "They don't want us wandering about on our own.

Whatever is going on here, they want to stop us finding out about it."

Charles held a finger to his lips and waved his free hand around the room.

"Bugs?" snorted Agatha. "They wouldn't dare. They know Toni swept this room and they wouldn't risk us doing it again and finding whatever they'd planted."

She rifled through the files that were stacked on the table, selected a couple and shoved the rest towards Charles.

"There are a few files that I've not had a good look at," she said, placing her handbag on the table and retrieving her cigarettes and lighter. "Why don't you take a squint at these and see if anything jumps out at you. I doubt it will. There's nothing much in them."

"Are you allowed to smoke in here?" asked Charles, raising an eyebrow.

"Yes, I *am,*" said Agatha, emphasising the word with a nod of her head. "There's never been any sort of problem with me smoking in here. They've even provided a couple of weird ashtray things."

"Yes, I noticed those," said Charles, picking one up to take a closer look. "You know what these are, don't you?"

"Ashtrays," said Agatha, "with . . . funny little lids."

106

"They are, of course, a pair of ashtrays, sweetie," said Charles, "but they have been made from the hooves of a horse."

"From what? Yeeoow!" Agatha wrinkled her nose, then quickly unwrinkled it for fear that the wrinkles might stay. "You mean they cut off a horse's feet just to . . . ?"

"Souvenirs, Aggie," Charles explained. "Mementoes. The Duke of Wellington's war horse, Copenhagen, had at least one hoof removed when he died. It was made into an ink stand. And then there was Wellington's arch enemy, Napoleon. When his horse, Marengo, died, one of his hooves was also made into an ink stand and another into a snuff box. The snuff box is in the Household Cavalry Museum at Horse Guards in White-hall."

"I suppose," said Agatha, lighting a cigarette, "your history degree does come in handy sometimes."

"It's not only the history thing," said Charles, who seldom admitted to having a degree, despite the fact that it was a first from Oxford. He weighed the ashtray in his hand. "I've seen plenty of these things around. These ones appear to have a weight added, probably lead in the base, to give them more substance. And the heavy silver decoration is quite nice." He turned the hoof over. "There's an inscription on the bottom. Apparently this hoof once won at Ascot while it was part of Lucky Lad."

"Not so lucky that he managed to avoid having his hooves lopped off," snorted Agatha.

"He would have been dead," said Charles, "so I doubt he would have cared much. There's a nice patina of age on this one, although the silver is tarnished," he added, setting the ashtray down on the table. "That one, on the other hand — or other hoof — has had all the character scrubbed out of it. It has been brutally cleaned." He reached across to examine the second ashtray.

"DON'T TOUCH IT!" cried Agatha. Charles whipped his hand away.

"Why ever not?"

"Because that, my dear Charles, is evidence. That thing was used to kill Mrs. Dinwiddy. It's not just a hoof or an ashtray — that is a murder weapon!"

"A murder weapon?" mused Charles. "Are you sure?"

"I am positive!" Agatha asserted, swelling with confidence, convinced that she had found the first and most important element of proof that Dinwiddy's death was indeed murder. "That hoof was not so squeaky clean when we were last in here. Whoever murdered her wanted to make it look like Wizz-Wazz did it, so they whacked her with that — a hoof — and then plastered the donkey's hooves with blood and dabbed some drops of blood on her hind legs for good measure. That's why one ashtray has been newly scrubbed. They have cleaned it to try to remove any trace of blood or anything else that would identify it as the murder weapon."

"A horse hoof," said Charles, considering her theory, "is a different shape to a donkey hoof."

"The killer must have wrapped it in a sock or something," said Agatha. "As long as it was roughly the right shape, it would do. There would be no point in whacking her with a shovel or a cosh or a brick. That would have looked totally wrong. No, this is what the murderer used."

She snatched her mobile phone out of her handbag and put in a call to Bill Wong.

"Good morning, Agatha," said Bill. "I was just about to phone you. You have no more bodies or bits of bodies for me today, I hope?"

"Actually," Agatha countered, "in a way, I do . . ."

She explained about the ultra-clean hoof in the conference room, and although Bill bravely attempted to argue that Mrs. Dinwiddy's death was an accident, he was no match for Agatha Raisin in full flow. She soon wore him down, leaving him, a bit like Lucky Lad, with barely a leg to stand on. He promised that he would be back at Morrison's himself later that morning to pick up the hoof for a forensic examination.

Agatha pushed a button to end the call and grinned in triumph at Charles.

"We mustn't touch it," she said. "Bill is coming to take it away. He's going to give it to their forensic people."

"Do you think they'll find anything on it?" Charles wondered. "It looks like it's been cleaned very thoroughly."

"They might," said Agatha, "but even if they don't, the simple fact that it has been cleaned so meticulously is suspicious in itself. I think this murder is starting to unravel, Charles. Now, let's see if we can have a little look around this place without an escort."

She crossed the room to the door and quietly eased it open. The corridor outside was silent and, as she'd expected, there was absolutely no one in sight.

"Where are we going?" whispered Charles, falling in behind as they sneaked along the corridor, hugging the wall.

"Wherever," Agatha replied in a hushed voice. "Dispatch, the old R&D, let's just take a look."

After a few yards, the corridor turned sharp left.

"Keep an eye out back there." Agatha jabbed a thumb over her shoulder, indicating behind them. "I'll see if the coast's clear this way."

Slowly she inched forward, craning her neck so that she could peer round the corner with just one eye. Then she stood statue still. Coming along the corridor ahead was Angus Bream. She turned and moved sharply back the way she had come. Unfortunately, Charles turned at precisely the same moment, and her right breast slammed into his elbow. She bounced off him, suffocating a squeal with "Mmmmmmmm!" and thinking: Bloody hell, that hurt! She staggered back, her arms flailing as though she were trying to swim through the air to regain her balance. Just as she thought she had it under control, her last rearward stumble snapped the shiny high heel of her left suede boot and she fell over, landing on her bottom with a resounding THUD! She skidded across the lino and came to a halt lying on her back in the wrong part of the corridor, massaging her throbbing boob.

"Need a hand with that, Mrs. Raisin?"

She opened her eyes to see the dusty black work boots and blue trouser legs of Angus Bream. He was sniggering. *Sniggering!* She left her sore breast alone. The pain from her battered bottom had almost cancelled it out anyway. Her first thought was to tell Bream to button his lip and help her up. Then again, if he thought this was a bit of a laugh and she was just an idiotic woman, why not use that?

"That would be very helpful," she squeaked, reaching out to him.

Charles was also at her side. He and Bream took a hand each and hoisted her to her feet.

"Are you all right, sweetie?" asked Charles.

"I'm fine, thanks," said Agatha, breathing heavily. "Just bruised my ar . . . dignity. Thank you, Mr. Bream."

"What were you doing here, Mrs. Raisin?" asked Bream.

"We were . . . going down to the stables," Agatha replied. "I left my best coat with that silly donkey and I wanted to get it back."

"I see," said Bream. "I'll take you down there, then. We wouldn't want you getting lost or falling over again, would we?"

Charles picked up the snapped heel and

handed it to Agatha. She gave him such a sweet smile that he knew something was up. Agatha would never ruin a prize pair of boots and simply act like nothing had happened. A smile of any kind would not grace her features for many days. Crying over spilled milk was as nothing compared to a wailing Agatha grieving over trashed footwear. She was up to something. He took the hint and meekly played along.

Flanked by the two men, Agatha walked along the corridor. On her right step she bobbed above their shoulders. On her left step she sank towards their elbows. Her right heel clicked; her left sole flopped. Click-flop, click-flop — it set an annoying rhythm as they walked.

"You know your way around here pretty well, then?" she asked Bream.

"That's my job, Mrs. Raisin."

"Is it much different to the place in Seky . . . Selky . . . Have you ever been there?"

"Sekiliv — and yes, I've been there a few times to check out security. It is very different. There are a handful of the staff from here based out there now. We even have our own courier service that runs once a week."

"A courier service?" asked Agatha. "What do you courier?"

"Sounds quite grand, doesn't it?" Bream laughed. "It's just a couple of blokes in a van, really. They bring different types of batteries, small orders, even the odd passenger coming home on holiday. On the way back, they take company papers, plans, and blueprints that the boss doesn't trust to go by email, and the odd jar of Branston Pickle or marmalade for the Brits working out there. I've done the van trip. It's a long slog and it can get hot and sweaty, but it's a real giggle."

"Sounds lovely," said Agatha, and with a few more click-flops they reached a staircase that took them down to the door she and Toni had used when they'd previously left the factory to visit the stables. As they stepped out of the main building, they heard a bleeping sound. Bream pulled a walkie-talkie from his pocket. He waved them towards the stables while he responded to the call, and Agatha recognised the voice of Farley Dunster through the radio's crackle of static.

They walked on past the R&D building and saw the grubby form of Peter Trotter in the stable yard, hosing down the cobbles and scrubbing them with a stiff broom.

"You!" Trotter spat when he saw Agatha hobbling towards him. "What are you doin' here?"

Agatha sniffed. There was a strong smell of bleach. Trotter was clearly using it to get rid of the bloodstains. She sidestepped a rivulet of water running off the cobbles. Her boots might be salvageable, but not if the pristine black suede was disfigured by bleach.

"I have come to retrieve my coat, which I left around Wizz-Wazz's neck," she said.

"Ha! You'll be lucky," scoffed Trotter. "The murdering bitch won't let me have it. She nearly took my hand off with those teeth of hers. Won't let me anywhere near her."

"Like pretty much every other female, I should think," said Agatha.

"Now listen here, you snooty cow . . ." Trotter pointed the broom handle at Agatha and advanced towards her. Charles took a step to cut him off, but Trotter paused, looking beyond Charles to where, out of the corner of her eye, Agatha could see Bream watching and shaking his head. "One day," Trotter sneered, "you'll get what's comin' to you."

"Do try to take a bath before then," said Agatha. "You smell worse than the donkey."

Trotter scuttled across the yard, opened the door of his old Land Rover, grabbed his copy of the *Racing Post* and headed up a set of wrought-iron stairs to his flat. Agatha selected a pristine carrot from the bucket and approached Wizz-Wazz's loose box. Feeding her a carrot hadn't worked out too well before, but she wanted something to tempt the donkey into giving up her jacket. It will need to be dry-cleaned, possibly fumigated, she thought, but I love that coat. What was I thinking of, giving it to that ridiculous animal?

She leaned over the loose box door to see Wizz-Wazz staring up at her with big watery eyes. You knew I was here, didn't you? Agatha thought. You heard my voice and you know I want my coat back, so now you're giving me the sad eyes and the long face. Or do you always have the long face? I suppose you can't exactly shorten it, can you?

"Don't look at me like that, my girl," she said aloud. "You know what I want. I'm offering a fair trade — carrot for coat."

Wizz-Wazz reached up and accepted the carrot. She began munching noisily and Agatha stretched in to take the jacket. Wizz-Wazz swayed effortlessly to one side, dodging just inches out of her reach. Agatha floundered at the door.

"Charles!" she called. "I could use a little help here."

Charles had a longer reach, but Wizz-Wazz

116

was surprisingly nimble.

"Agatha," said Charles, making another fruitless attempt to retrieve the coat, "I've been meaning to talk to you about —"

"Concentrate, Charles!" Agatha chided. "Oh, it's no good. You'll have to go in there with the beast."

"Hello," came a familiar voice. They both turned to see Toni standing there. Bream was walking away, obviously having escorted her to the stables. Toni stared at Charles, who had a sudden cold feeling of foreboding. He hasn't told her, she thought. All Charles could think was: Toni *knows*!

"Toni," said Agatha. "About time. Come over here and help me get my coat back. What were you about to say, Charles?"

"Ah, yes," said Charles. "Not really the time or place . . . but you see, er . . . there's someone you should meet. Yes, that's it. You said you wanted to find out more about this electric car business, and I know just the chap you should talk to. He's an engineer or mechanic or whatever. Rents some barn space from me on the estate, down by the ford. Chris . . . Chris something-or-other. I'll let him know you're coming. Must dash." And with that, he rushed off.

"What's got into him?" said Agatha, removing herself from the loose box door and brushing stray bits of straw off her raincoat.

"I really couldn't say," Toni replied.

There came a light clatter of latch metal from behind Agatha, and the loose box door swung ominously open. Wizz-Wazz stepped forward out of the shadows.

"Look out, Agatha!" Toni squealed. "It's got out again!"

Running in smooth-soled boots with one heel missing was not an option, and neither, Agatha suddenly felt, was it at all necessary. She calmly stood her ground as Wizz-Wazz sidled up to her. The donkey gently tucked her head under Agatha's arm and gave a contented chuckle.

"It seems to like you," said Toni.

"I can't think why," Agatha grimaced, turning her face away from the almost overpowering and peculiarly dry smell of donkey. "Apart from the fact that I gave her a rather nice, rather expensive coat." Looking at the jacket in daylight, she could see that amongst its once luxurious red fur there now nestled a carpet of straw fragments and assorted other debris, most of which she chose not to try to identify. It was revolting. "And I think she can keep it."

"So what's the plan for today?" Toni asked.

"Well, I'm really rather bored with this place," said Agatha, absent-mindedly stroking Wizz-Wazz's ears. "They're keeping too close an eye on us for us to turn up anything here. Let's go and see the grease monkey Charles was talking about. Come on, you," she added, leading Wizz-Wazz towards her stall. "Back inside."

Toni fell in beside Agatha as she click-flopped out of the stable yard.

"I'd say you were getting to like that donkey," she said, "if I didn't know you better."

"You will never know me better, dear," said Agatha. "I am a woman of infinite mystery."

"What happened to your boot?"

"That's another of my mysteries."

Agatha reached back and gently ran her hand across her aching behind. There was definitely going to be bruising.

Sir Charles Fraith's estate extended to over a thousand acres of arable land, mainly worked by tenant farmers. Toni knew exactly where the old ford was. A narrow lane to the south of the estate was bisected by a stream with neither bridge for the road nor tunnel for the water. Splashing through the ford had been fun with a buzz of risk thrown in. What if the car conked out? It hadn't, but that relationship inevitably had. Another failed romance.

"Cheer up, Toni!" said Agatha. "Look — the sun's coming out. We haven't seen much sunshine for days. It makes everything feel better, doesn't it?" Except, perhaps, my bottom, she thought, as the car bounced over a pothole.

"I think this is it," Toni said, pulling the car off the lane by a collection of old farm buildings. The wide doors of one of the barns stood open and a man in oil-stained grey overalls emerged. Agatha hopped out of the car and hobbled round to meet him.

"Good morning, ladies." The man smiled. "What can I do for you?" He was of medium height, with a slim build and a shock of dark wavy hair, going slightly grey at the sides. Agatha swiftly assessed him at mid- to late-forties. He had a strong jaw and his smile etched comfortable creases into his handsome face. All of that she captured in one glimpse, but she could not drag her gaze away from the man's eyes. They were the most astonishing, vibrant blue. She was captivated.

"We are looking for Chris . . . something-

120

or-other." She beamed her brightest smile at him.

"Firkin."

"What?"

"Chris Firkin," said the man. "That's me. You must be Agatha. Sir Charles phoned to say you were coming." He snapped off a blue latex glove and held out his hand. Agatha reached to shake it. It was a strong hand, and quite the cleanest she had ever seen attached to a mechanic. Whenever she had needed to have any work done on her car, the garage staff appeared to have years of oil and grime embedded in the skin on their hands. And their fingernails — mechanics must be born with black fingernails. It was the only explanation. Chris Firkin's hand, however, was unsullied by even the hint of an oily blemish.

Firkin politely shook hands with Toni and then turned back to Agatha, noting her lopsided stance. He looked down at her heel-less boot.

"What's happened to you?" he asked.

"That? A bit of a wardrobe malfunction," Agatha laughed, waving a hand dismissively. "It's nothing."

"I think we can do something about that," he said, kneeling at her feet to inspect the damaged boot. "Do you have the broken

121

heel? Hold on a second." He hurried back into the barn and returned an instant later carrying a pair of pristine white tennis shoes.

"You mustn't walk on those boots," he said, kneeling at her feet once again. "You'll damage them both. Try these." He grasped Agatha first by one knee and ankle and then the other, gently supporting her while he slipped her boots off and planted her feet in his own tennis shoes.

"Those will do you for the moment," he said, examining the broken heel. "Yes, we can soon sort this out. It will take a little while for the glue to dry, though."

No sooner had he turned his back than Agatha had slipped out of her raincoat and reapplied her lipstick in what seemed like one fluid movement. Toni reckoned that any stage conjuror would have been impressed. Where had the lipstick suddenly appeared from?

"Well, Toni," said Agatha in a voice loud enough for Firkin to hear. "I don't think you need wait around. Why don't you go back to the office and organise the troops for a case conference tomorrow morning?" Then she added in a whisper, "How do I look?"

Toni grinned at her boss standing in the sunshine in a bright red Preen dress with perfectly matching lipstick, her raincoat folded neatly over one arm and massive white tennis shoes on her feet. Agatha Raisin on the make was a sight to be admired.

"You look amazing." She nodded. "See you tomorrow."

Agatha shuffled off towards the barn, following Firkin. Inside was an entire workshop, lit by a low-hanging neon light. A forest of tools lined the walls, hanging in neat rows, each in its own space. For what most of them might be used, Agatha could scarcely guess, although some had the look of instruments of torture. In the centre of the space stood an old Volkswagen camper van. Its immaculate paintwork was a gleaming ruby red below a swoop of white that ran from the front up onto the roof all the way to the rear. Agatha made her way the length of the vehicle. At the back, where she was fairly certain there should be an engine, there was a gaping hole.

"Unfinished electric conversion," explained Firkin, applying glue to Agatha's boot. "It's what I do. Turn knackered old classic cars into modern electric vehicles."

"Ah," said Agatha. "That's why Charles recommended that I meet you." She leant casually against the camper, slid off its

123

glossy paintwork and quickly readjusted her stance.

"Yes," said Firkin, setting the boot to one side. "I did some consultancy work for Morrison's. It will be extraordinary if they can get that battery pack to work."

"You don't think they can?"

"They are having problems. Fancy a coffee?"

From a storeroom he brought a car's rear bench seat and set it in the sunshine outside his workshop. He and Agatha sat down with mugs of fresh coffee.

"Why won't they get it to work?" asked Agatha.

"Basically," Firkin began, "their battery is what everyone wants. It would give an electric car the same range as a petrol car. But a petrol car can be quickly refuelled, and in the past an electric car has taken hours to recharge. Nobody wants to have to wait around for ages while their battery recharges. So we now have rapid chargers appearing at filling stations and supermarkets that can do the job in a little over half an hour. You can recharge while you have a coffee or do your shopping. The big problem is that Morrison's battery pack can't cope with rapid charging."

"What do you mean, it can't cope?"

"Remember a few years ago when the airlines banned certain mobile phones because the batteries overheated and caused a fire hazard? That's what happens to the Morrison's pack on a rapid charger."

"You mean it could burst into flames?"

"Not just *could.* It did. Frequently."

"So was that what caused the fire that gutted the R&D department?"

"I was no longer working for the company at that time," said Firkin, "but I'm pretty sure that's what must have happened."

So it wasn't saboteurs, Agatha thought. The fire was started by Morrison's dodgy battery pack.

"Now," he said. "What about a spot of lunch?" He stood and stripped off his overalls. Underneath he was wearing neat blue chinos and a white polo shirt with a crest on the left breast.

"I'm not properly dressed for going out." Agatha smiled, waggling her feet in the tennis shoes.

"Your boots will be ready now." He disappeared inside to collect them. "I know an excellent little pub just the other side of Chipping Norton. Good food."

Agatha slipped on her boots and cocked her head towards the camper.

"Your van thing doesn't have an engine,"

she said.

"We're not going in that," said Firkin, locking the workshop doors. "We'll take the one round the corner."

Agatha's face fell as she walked round to where he had parked his VW Beetle. It had none of the glamour of the shiny camper. Its paint was a dull grey and it had been stripped of all its chrome trim. Inside, there were no carpets and a lot of the same dull grey metal. But it was remarkably clean.

"Don't worry, it's perfectly sound and roadworthy," said Firkin. "It just needs a little finishing, that's all."

Agatha eased herself slowly into the passenger seat, hiding a slight wince when her bruised backside achieved touchdown, and they set off, gliding out into the lane in total silence.

"I thought these cars made a kind of noisy spluttering," she said, raising her eyebrows.

"Electric motor." Firkin grinned. "Smooth and quiet."

"And it's all very neat in here," said Agatha. "My cars tend to be an extension of my . . ."

"Glamorous personality?" offered Firkin. "Elegant good looks?"

". . . handbag."

They were stopped at traffic lights towards

the outskirts of Chipping Norton when Agatha became aware of a balding man in a red sports car sitting alongside them. She watched him appraise the Beetle with a sneer, and then he waggled his eyebrows at her. Her immediate reaction was to hoist a finger at him, but she managed to stop herself just in time. Firkin saw what was happening and laughed.

"Shall we teach him a lesson?" he said.

The lights changed to green and the Beetle shot forward. Agatha's head snapped back and she could feel her body being pushed into the back of the seat. The electric motor made a high-pitched hum, like a TV spaceship. The fancy sports car was left grumbling in their wake.

"You see," said Firkin. "He has to go through his gears and hit the right revs to achieve maximum torque for top acceleration. Whereas an electric motor produces maximum torque all the time and —"

"Enough torque talk," said Agatha, holding up a hand. "This is just quicker. Electric quick."

"Spot-on," nodded Firkin, laughing.

In the pub, they settled at a cosy table by the window and enjoyed the last of the fast-fading warmth of the sun through the glass.

They ate excellent fish and chips, flaky cod cooked in a delicate beer batter that started off crispy then simply melted in the mouth. Agatha washed it down with several glasses of dry white wine, while Firkin, as driver, limited himself to one.

They lingered far too long, whiling away most of the afternoon. Agatha questioned Firkin mercilessly about his entire life. He had been in the Royal Navy, in submarines. He had been married, but as he put it, "Being away so much made things difficult. We grew apart. Absence does not always make the heart grow fonder."

It was beginning to get dark by the time the little electric car cruised noiselessly along Lilac Lane to Agatha's cottage. Firkin stopped, as directed, at the gate.

"That was fun," she said. "We must do it again."

"Definitely," he agreed. "How about Friday? Dinner?"

"It's a date." She smiled, and leaned over to give him a peck on the cheek, but he turned his head and their lips met instead.

"That was a fast move," she said, pulling away.

"Electric quick," said Firkin.

She moved closer and kissed him again, more slowly, a lingering, passionate kiss.

128

"That was a slow move," he said. "I liked it better. I will pick you up on Friday evening."

Agatha skipped up her garden path with a spring in her step. Today, she thought, had turned into a very successful day. Roll on Friday.

CHAPTER FIVE

The following morning, having given the cats their breakfast, Agatha sat at her kitchen table, savouring a cup of delicious coffee without her customary cigarette. Romance was in the air and today, she decided, was a good day to start afresh and kick the habit. She smiled at the way the cats' tails formed big fluffy question marks when they were happy. If I had a tail, she thought, I would be doing the same with it right now. Instead, I've got a bottom that's turning black and blue. That would never happen to Hodge or Boswell. If ever they did anything as undignified as falling from the back of the sofa or the garden fence, they always managed to land on their feet and act as if they meant it all along.

"But you two don't have to wear high heels, do you?" she said out loud, laughing as the cats looked up at her with big eyes, apparently aghast at the very thought. Just then there was a knock at the door. "Who could that be, guys? Early-morning visitors two days in a row?"

She covered the tiny hallway in a few strides and opened the door to find Doris Simpson, her trusty cleaning lady, standing there.

"You're a bit early today, aren't you, Doris?" she said, stepping aside to let the cleaner in. "And it's Saturday. This isn't your day."

"Ah, yes, sorry about that," Doris apologised, "but my cousin Rita has put her back out and I need to get over to Evesham to stay with her for a couple of days, so I thought I'd ask if you wouldn't mind me doing you today instead of Monday."

"I suppose that's okay. You should have just let yourself in." Agatha returned to the kitchen and her morning coffee. "You have keys."

"Well, I weren't sure," said Doris, "whether you might be entertaining your new gentleman friend."

Agatha's eyebrows climbed up her forehead. Chris had brought her home as it was getting dark in a car that didn't make a sound, and Doris knew about it by the very next morning. MI5 could take a few tips from the way the Carsely village spy network gleaned information. Obviously the real reason she had turned up early was to try to catch a glimpse of Agatha's "new man." The first person to have a description of him would be in possession of a gossip gold card.

"But as you can see," Agatha said, indicating the single coffee cup on the table, "I'm not. Tell me, Doris, do you know anyone who works at Morrison's?"

"Not really," said Doris. "Not a very big place, is it? Batteries or something, I think. My husband's cousin's girl Tracey was there for a while but she packed it in. Too many people there that she didn't like."

"How long ago was that?" asked Agatha. "Did she know Josie, the receptionist?"

"Oh, she knew her all right." Doris laughed. "Everyone knew Josie and what she got up to with that Albert Morrison. Tracey has some stories to tell about that."

"What happened to Josie?"

"She walked out one day saying she were never coming back. Tracey said she saw her with her handbag stuffed full of cash. Said Josie was obsessed with that film *South Pacific.* She watched it over and over. Even went to see the stage show up in London. She told Tracey she was off to discover paradise, then trashed the reception desk, and danced out the front door singing 'I'm Gonna Wash That Man Right Outa My Hair.' "

Just then there came another knock at the door. Agatha took one last sip of her coffee and made for the hall once again.

"Good morning," she said brightly, finding Toni on the doorstep. "I wasn't expecting you this morning. I thought we'd meet at the office."

"I know," said Toni, stepping into the hall, "but I thought you might like a lift . . . and I wanted to talk to you about something before we got to the office. It's, well . . . How did things go yesterday?"

"I had a very nice, very informative afternoon," said Agatha, "but you didn't have to come here to ask me about —"

There was yet another knock. Unbelievable, thought Agatha. Who on earth was it this time? This time it was Bill Wong, accompanied by Alice Peterson.

"Morning, Agatha," he said. "Mind if we come in?"

"Why not?" said Agatha. "Everyone else has."

The cramped hall of her cottage left little room for manoeuvre, especially when Doris appeared with the vacuum cleaner.

"Living room," said Agatha, waving Alice

and Bill through the door. "Doris, you can start upstairs. Toni, would you be a dear and make us all some fresh coffee?"

Bill and Alice sat down on Agatha's sofa while she perched on the arm of a chair. She had things to do today and she was anxious to give the impression that they were not settling in for very long. She winced as her bruised bottom complained about the hard chair arm and gently lowered herself into the cushion instead.

"Did you find anything on the hoof?" she asked Bill.

"Not a thing," he said. "It had recently been scrubbed with chemical cleaners. There were no fingerprints on it, nothing that could be used in evidence."

"Except the fact that it had been scrubbed," said Agatha. "Why had that hoof been cleaned so well and not the other one?"

"According to Bream at the factory," said Alice, "it was given a good clean because someone had been smoking and used it. You, I think."

"Ridiculous!" snorted Agatha. "You *empty* an ashtray and give it a wipe when it has been used. You don't scrub it almost out of existence!"

"I agree that is strange," said Bill, "and I don't much like some of those characters at

Morrison's, but we have no real evidence to suggest that the death of Mrs. Dinwiddy was anything other than what it appears to be — an accident. We need to take a formal statement from you now, as the person who discovered the body. We spoke to Toni yesterday."

"What's the rush?" asked Agatha, frowning.

"Chief Inspector Wilkes wants everything tied up before the inquest," Alice explained.

"Which is when?" Agatha demanded.

"This afternoon," said Bill, "at two o'clock."

"You have to be joking!" cried Agatha. "Whoever heard of an inquest on a Saturday?"

"It's not normal procedure," Bill confirmed, "but this has been deemed a very straightforward accident — an easy case to deal with and get out of the way. The chief inspector wants it all done and dusted. He says we don't have the time or the budget to waste on this. The coroner agreed to fit us in today providing that we had everything in order. All we need now is a statement from you."

"Well, here's my statement," said Agatha, her voice strained, her jaw taut. "Wilkes is a pillock!"

Alice, who had been sitting with pen and paper at the ready, covered her mouth to hide a giggle. Bill rubbed his temples and sighed.

"That's not very helpful, Agatha," he said.

"Helpful?" cried Agatha, jumping to her feet. "What would be *helpful* is if you were allowed to conduct a proper investigation into what the hell is going on at Morrison's that led to a woman being MURDERED!"

"Calm down, Agatha," said Toni, arriving with a tray of coffee cups. "You're getting yourself into a state. Why don't you have a cigarette?"

"BECAUSE I'VE GIVEN UP!" Agatha roared.

The others looked at each other and nodded wisely.

"Don't you patronise me," said Agatha, settling back into her seat and scanning the room with an accusing finger. "I have every right to be upset when I discovered the body of a murdered woman and Wilkes is prepared to let the bastards get away with it."

"So who *is* getting away with it?" asked Bill.

"I don't know yet," Agatha replied, "but I intend to find out."

Accepting a cup of coffee from Toni, she ran through a short version of the events leading to the discovery in the stable yard. She paused when she came to the part where she saw Dinwiddy's body lying on the ground and Wizz-Wazz standing by her. Something was missing from that picture and she had yet to figure out what.

Driving to the office in Mircester, Agatha and Toni were finally alone.

"So what was it you wanted to talk about?" Agatha asked. "Have you figured out what to do about that young man of yours?"

"You know, that really is my business. I don't need you interfering."

"Who's interfering? I have your best interests at heart," said Agatha, thinking to herself: and I don't want you lumbering yourself with a demanding husband and a pack of squalling kids when I need you in the office.

"I am perfectly able to deal with my own private life," said Toni.

"Good," Agatha responded, "because you don't want to go falling head over heels for the first thing that comes along in trousers."

"Or overalls?"

"That was *low!*"

They looked away from each other, then slowly turned back and both burst out laughing.

"He's really very nice," said Agatha.

"He looked it," said Toni. "I'm pleased for you." Now was not the time to tell her about Charles.

Agatha settled behind her desk at Raisin Investigations, Toni and Patrick Mulligan filing into the room behind her. They sat opposite her, both wielding notebooks and pens.

"Right," said Agatha. "Let's share what we know about the Morrison's affair. First, we need to know the people we are dealing with. What have you got, Toni?"

"I've done a bit of digging into Aphrodite Morrison's past," said Toni, "and it's been a real eye-opener. She is thirty years old and was born here as Kate Hibbert. Her mother was English and her father was an American serviceman, an engine fitter with the US Air Force. They never married. He was posted back to the States and Kate was brought up here by her mother. When Kate was just seventeen, her mother died and she headed to the States to track down her father. She never found him, but she was a beautiful young woman and soon found work as a model in New York."

"I could have guessed," Agatha nodded,

"by the way she dresses."

"Dressing," said Toni, "was not a major requirement for the kind of modelling she was doing. She was known by a number of names, including Adorable Angelica from Arkansas, Lusty Layla from Louisiana and . . . I'm not even going to mention the Kentucky one.

"Five years ago, she got married to a billionaire Wall Street broker, Edwin Levin. The marriage lasted only nine months before he died. She inherited over a hundred million dollars."

"A-ha!" said Agatha. "That sounds like a pretty suspicious death!"

"Not really," Toni explained. "He was ninety-two. He told reporters when they got engaged that he wanted to go out with a bang."

Patrick Mulligan let out a wheezing laugh. "Any photos of Lusty Layla?" he asked.

"None at all," said Toni. "Edwin bought up every photo of her and had teams scouring the internet to acquire and destroy any images. He wanted her all to himself.

"His family — he had children from previous marriages — contested the will, but Kate, who had by then changed her name to Aphrodite, still walked away with a large share of the Levin millions. She met Albert

Morrison at a hotel in Saint-Tropez three years ago and they were married within six months."

Agatha sat back in her chair. "Wow," she said. "Our Aphrodite's quite a girl, isn't she? What have you got on Morrison, Patrick?"

"He's not nearly as interesting as his wife," said Mulligan. "He's forty-eight. An only child. Comes from a middle-class family. Has a degree in chemical engineering. Worked for a few of the big corporations before he took over the family business when his father died thirteen years ago. He set up the plant in Sekiliv. He has no kids, and as Toni said, he married Aphrodite three years ago."

"He's so dull," Agatha moaned. "Whatever did Aphrodite see in him?"

"A father figure maybe," offered Toni. "Someone to look after her, make her feel secure."

"Could be." Agatha nodded. "Now, what do we have on Morrison's security guards, Bream and Dunster?"

"As you suspected," said Mulligan, "neither of them was ever in the SAS, but they were both in the army, in the Royal Logistics Corps."

"What's that?" asked Agatha.

"It's the biggest army corps. They supply

and transport everything from food and clothes to fuel and ammunition. Bream and Dunster served together in Germany and in Afghanistan. A mate of mine in the Royal Military Police told me that there was a real scandal involving their unit in Germany. All sorts of stuff was going missing by the truckload — petrol, clothing, food, booze, you name it. It all stopped when the unit was shipped out to Afghanistan, and the military police never got to the bottom of it.

"Bream went AWOL — absent without leave — in Afghanistan for three weeks. He then spent two months in a military prison before being kicked out of the army. Dunster was also dismissed from Her Majesty's Service. He picked a fight with another squaddie and ended up breaking his legs with a crowbar. He's a nasty piece of work."

"So Dunster has a vicious streak," Agatha pondered, "and he and Bream have clearly kept in touch."

"Not just kept in touch," said Mulligan. "They worked together in a warehouse in Leicester but were sacked after they got into a fight with the foreman. He found out they had been running some kind of mail order business of their own out of his warehouse. Police were called. After that, there's nothing on them until they both turned up here."

"Why would Morrison's want to employ two thugs like Bream and Dunster?" Toni wondered.

"That's another question for John Sayer," said Agatha. "What do you have on him?"

"Nothing yet," Mulligan admitted. "He's a bit of a puzzle. I can only think that perhaps John Sayer is not his real name. I'm working on it."

"Good," said Agatha. "We need to know how the mysterious Mr. Sayer fits in. Keep at it, Patrick. Now," she added, "I can fill you in on what I discovered yesterday. Mr. Sayer was not entirely truthful with us about the staff in Sekiliv. There are some Brits working out there . . ."

She explained about the courier service, and how Josie appeared to have been paid off to get her out of the way.

". . . and then there's the battery pack," she continued. "It doesn't work. In fact, it's downright dangerous. It has a tendency to burst into flames. That's almost certainly what caused the fire."

"So we were right," said Toni. "We were being used to make Morrison's look like they had something to protect, to cover up the fact that their battery is useless. Then the leg stunt was to discredit us so that we could be dispensed with."

"That's looking most likely now," Agatha agreed. "We can probably expect to have our contract with Morrison's cancelled any time now. We'll have to move fast if we are to get to the bottom of this."

"And we still don't know *why* Dinwiddy was murdered," Mulligan pointed out. "Unless she found out what was going on."

"She knew there were problems with the battery pack," Agatha reasoned, "but there were others who knew that, too. Chris Firkin for one. No, Dinwiddy believed that the battery's teething problems were being resolved, so why kill her? There has to be something more."

"She could have found out about the boss and the receptionist," Mulligan suggested.

"Without a doubt," said Agatha, "but that appears to have been fairly common knowledge."

"And it was dealt with in any case," said Toni. "Josie was got rid of — paid off."

"We're still not seeing the full picture." Agatha sighed.

"But we are making progress," said Mulligan. "You found the murder weapon."

"And we have a list of suspects," said Toni. "Albert Morrison may have been having an affair with Dinwiddy. If she had become an inconvenience, he might have wanted rid of her."

"Then there's Farley and Dunster," added Mulligan. "Dinwiddy seemed wary of them. Maybe they had some kind of grudge against her. And Sayer. We don't know enough about him yet."

"We should consider Aphrodite, too," Toni said. "She might have found out about Morrison's affair with Dinwiddy and decided to bump her off."

"But all of those," argued Agatha, "have cast-iron alibis. We saw them all at the party at Morrison's house. They couldn't have reached the stable, clobbered Dinwiddy and vanished again before we arrived. We would have seen something. Wait, though . . . what about that vile little turd Peter Trotter?"

"He's a failed jockey," said Mulligan, consulting his notes. "Known to the police. Bar brawls mainly. Never held down a job for long. Can't think what his motive would be."

"He wouldn't need one," said Agatha. "He's got a real temper. He might just have flipped."

"That doesn't really fit, though," said Toni. "He couldn't have lost his temper, gone into the main building, retrieved the hoof ashtray and battered Dinwiddy, then framed the donkey, cleaned the hoof and returned it to the conference room."

"Agreed," said Mulligan. "This was premeditated. Whoever did it planned it in advance and had the ashtray ready to use."

"Trotter is too thick for that." Agatha nodded. "He couldn't plan his way into a clean pair of underpants."

"And he also has an alibi," Toni said. "According to Bill Wong, he walked to the betting shop in Mircester and was seen leaving there with just enough time to get back for when we saw him arrive at the stables."

"Well, let's keep him on our list anyway," said Agatha. "I've no doubt that he's capable of murder." She slipped off her high heels and produced from a desk drawer a pair of flat shoes that Toni had never seen before. "Patrick," she said. "You stay on John Sayer. Toni, get yourself something to eat. I am going for a walk."

"A walk?" said Toni. "You mean to a pub for lunch?"

"Not at all," said Agatha, patting her stomach and sucking it in at the same time. "I am taking a little exercise. I can do without lunch, and if I went to the pub, I would have to have a drink, which might . . ."

"Make you want a cigarette?"

". . . cloud my thinking for this afternoon's inquest. I will see you back here in good time for that."

From the office window, Toni watched Agatha march briskly up the lane towards Mircester High Street, swinging her arms. Agatha Raisin on a health kick? That could only mean one thing. She was preparing for an all-out assault. Chris Firkin didn't stand a chance.

The coroner's inquest was held in a council chamber inside Mircester Town Hall, a building that dominated an open square in the centre of town. A short flight of steps led up to a double entrance door that sheltered beneath a triangular roof supported by two stone columns, a Victorian take on classical Greek architecture. It was, Agatha decided, failing in its attempt to impress. She had never paid the building much attention in the past and would pay it less in the future.

Bland wooden panelling lined the walls of the council chamber, and the room was laid out with rows of chairs, all facing a raised platform on which stood a desk decorated with the same featureless wood. A portly old man in a tweed suit sat behind the desk, and to his left, at a smaller desk, sat another

146

man, a clerk, almost hidden behind a computer screen.

Agatha and Toni took seats near the middle of the room. There were very few others in attendance. Albert Morrison sat to their left, near the front, flanked by Aphrodite and John Sayer. Several rows behind them was an elderly couple, the woman demurely dressed in a sombre black coat and the man unremarkable save for a glorious crown of curly silver-grey hair.

To Agatha's right, she could see the backs of Chief Inspector Wilkes, Bill Wong, and Dr. Charles Bunbury. She recognised none of the handful of others in the room.

The coroner said a few words to get proceedings under way and asked a few questions of Wilkes, who stood to give concise, direct answers. He then questioned Dr. Bunbury, who, Agatha could tell, was enjoying being the centre of attention.

". . . and it is my considered opinion," he droned, "supported by a weight of indisputable evidence, that death was caused by . . ."

"Yes, yes, we have all that," mumbled the coroner, interrupting by waving a sheaf of papers. "Blow to the back of the head and so on . . ."

The hearing had been in progress for only twenty minutes when, to Agatha's surprise, the coroner began drawing things to a close. Was there really to be no more discussion, no more investigation? The death of Mrs. Dinwiddy, she thought, was being dispensed with in inappropriate haste.

"Fwom the evidence that has been pwesented to me and the testimonies given to this inquest," burbled the coroner in a voice that spoke of a heavy lunch followed by too many glasses of port — the port, Agatha decided, might also have aggravated his inability to pronounce the letter *R* — "I am of the opinion that the death of Mrs. Clawissa Dinwiddy was the wesult of a twagic incident when the donkey known as Wishy-Washy . . ."

The clerk leant over and whispered something.

". . . the donkey known as Wizz-Wazz lashed out with its back hooves. The injuwies sustained by Mrs. Dinwiddy pwoved to be fatal. Death was almost instantaneous. My conclusion is that this was an accidental death."

"That is utter nonsense!" cried Agatha, shooting from her seat. "This was no accident!"

"And you aw, madam . . . ?" said the coroner, looking at her over the top of his spectacles.

148

"I am Agatha Raisin, private investigator."

"Is this woman known to you, Chief Inspectoh?" the coroner asked, turning to Wilkes.

"She is indeed, sir," said Wilkes, standing to respond and casting a furious glare towards Agatha. If looks could kill, she thought, they'd be booking another inquest around now. Bill Wong stared straight ahead. "She discovered the body and —"

"Ah, yes," said the coroner, sifting through the papers in front of him and dismissing Wilkes with a wave of his hand. "The one who was pweviously attacked by the donkey."

"That wasn't an attack," said Agatha. "That was just Wizz-Wazz being . . . playful."

"Playful, you say? Yet you fled fwom the animal in gweat distwess."

"I did not *flee*," said Agatha indignantly. "I just . . . didn't know Wizz-Wazz very well then, so we decided to keep our distance."

"Vewwy wise. Had you attempted to befwiend the beast, you might well be the subject of this inquest instead of Mrs. Dinwiddy. That donkey is a dangewous animal that caused a fatal accident."

"Oh, don't be so ridiculous! This was not an accident — it was murder!"

"Mrs. Waisin! I will thank you not to take that tone with me. You should know that a donkey cannot commit mudah. Only people can commit mudah."

"Of course I know that! Wizz-Wazz wasn't the murderer, you silly old fool!"

"What? What did you . . . !? Have this woman wemoved at once!"

"I'm going!" said Agatha, seeing two officials in grey suits closing in on her. "But you haven't heard the last of this!"

"And I wecommend," she heard the coroner pronounce just as she and Toni reached the door, "that the donkey should be destwoyed."

"You can't do that!" she yelled, turning back to the room. "WIZZ-WAZZ IS INNOCENT!!"

Every face in the council chamber was now turned towards her. She raised a clenched fist and repeated, "WIZZ-WAZZ IS INNOCENT!!" One of the grey suits reached for her arm. Agatha snatched it away. "Try that again," she snarled in a low voice, "and I'll rip your throat out." The man backed away.

Standing on the town hall steps staring out into the square, her heart pounding, seething with anger, Agatha suddenly craved a cigarette more than anything else in the world. No, she told herself. Those bastards in there are not going to beat me, and neither is smoking! I will fight them all! She heard a phone ring and saw, out of the corner of her eye, Toni taking the call on her mobile. A voice came from behind her.

" 'Wizz-Wazz is innocent.' That's a catchy slogan."

A slightly built young woman with dark hair and black-rimmed spectacles stepped into her line of sight. "Charlotte Clark," she introduced herself, clasping a reporter's notepad. *"Mircester Telegraph."*

"Yes . . . yes, that's exactly what it will be," said Agatha, her old instincts from her years spent in PR suddenly clicking into place. "Our slogan for the Save Wizz-Wazz campaign. We are not going to let that poor donkey take the blame for this foul murder!"

"You said that in the council chamber," said Clark. "Murder? What makes you think it was murder?"

"I have many, many reasons for thinking that," said Agatha. "Believe me, Miss Clark, this was murder and Wizz-Wazz is being framed for it."

Chief Inspector Wilkes came striding down the steps, his long legs taking them two at a time. "Whatever that woman is telling you," he sneered, "is utter claptrap. She is a fantasist, desperate for attention. Quite mad." And without pausing, he loped past.

"He's really not getting laid enough, is he?" said Agatha.

"Or even at all," Clark giggled.

"He can't stop us, though," Agatha affirmed. "We are going to save Wizz-Wazz."

"You's got me wid ya on that!" Aphrodite clacked down the steps on unfeasibly high heels with a balance and poise that drew Agatha's grudging admiration. "You ain't gonna let them execute my Wizz-Wazz, is you, Mrs. Raisin?"

"You have my word," Agatha said, watching Aphrodite effect a pitiful sob and dab a tissue at a completely tearless eye. "Why don't we launch our campaign at the stables on Monday morning?"

"You got it," Aphrodite said. "Anythin' you want, talk to him." She jabbed a thumb towards Sayer, who stood, as always, at Albert Morrison's side. Sayer smiled and nodded at Agatha. Morrison ignored her entirely, leading his wife off towards where Dunster waited with their car.

"That was an interesting performance," said Clark.

"She's an interesting woman." Agatha nodded. "You must come along to our campaign launch. It will be a great story."

"I already have a great story," said Clark, waving her notebook. " 'Killer Donkey Sentenced to Death. Chaos at Inquest. Private Eye Screams Murder.' I can make the front page of tomorrow's special edition."

This girl is a shrewd cookie, thought Agatha, but I need to keep control of how the publicity plays out now. This could be good for me, good for the business, and a great way to keep us involved at Morrison's.

"You could get that front page," said Agatha, "but I will level with you. I want to keep this under control. It's only going to get bigger. I think we can get the nationals involved, but they won't like it if you've beaten them to it. I need you to hold the story for now and pick it up along with everyone else on Monday."

"Why would I want to do that?" asked the girl. "What's in it for me?"

"This is going to be a story that has glamour, money, sex, a poor victimised donkey, and a murder," said Agatha. "And I will be at the centre of it all. When it's all over, you can have an exclusive. A one-on-one interview — the whole story. All the big boys will want it. It will be syndicated throughout the country and it will hit the newsstands in New York, too — all with your name on the byline."

"I will hold you to this," said Clark, tucking her notepad away.

I bet you will too, thought Agatha as the reporter walked away. Well, it would be worth it. She slid her hand across her stomach. A strange feeling. Hunger? No — excitement. You are buzzing, Agatha Raisin, like you did when you sat in the centre of a PR web in London, horse-trading with editors on newspaper picture desks, cajoling feature writers and bullying reporters. "You can have an exclusive" — when was the last time she had said that? Where was Toni? Still fiddling with her phone. What was she up to?

The woman in the black coat was standing just beyond Toni, her pale features turned towards Agatha. She took a couple of paces forward and said in a quiet voice, "Might I have a word with you, Mrs. Raisin?" Her grey eyes were filled with tears, but she was stubbornly refusing to allow even a single drop to fall.

"Of course," said Agatha. "How can I help?"

"I am Elizabeth Thirkettle," said the woman, "and this is my husband, Clive. I am Clarissa Dinwiddy's sister."

"I am so sorry about your sister," said Agatha, shaking the older woman's hand, "and I apologise if anything I said in there caused you any further upset."

"Not at all, my dear. In fact, you are the only one who is taking Clarissa's death seriously. You see, I agree with you. I too believe that my sister was murdered."

"You do? Why is that? Is there something you want to tell me, Mrs. Thirkettle?"

"Not here," said the woman, her eyes darting warily left and right. "Come to my house on Monday afternoon. Our address . . ."

She reached out to shake hands once again, and Agatha felt a neatly folded piece of paper being pressed into her palm. Clive Thirkettle also shook hands, his silver curls dipping forward as he nodded, then springing neatly back into place.

"Agatha," called Toni, holding up her phone. "Patrick's on to something. He sent me a photo. He'll have more by the time we get back to the office."

"Let's go then," said Agatha. Now things were really starting to move.

Agatha was invigorated with the thrill of the chase, and Toni struggled to keep up as she pounded the pavement all the way back to the office. When they arrived, Patrick was waiting by Toni's desk.

"I should have it on my screen," Toni said, sitting and tapping at her keyboard. "Here's the photo you sent."

A formal picture of a detachment of soldiers flickered onto the screen, front rows sitting, back rows standing, all wearing dark berets and dusky green-and-beige desert camouflage.

"This is Bream and Dunster's unit photographed in Afghanistan," said Mulligan.

"That's them," Agatha pointed, "in the back row."

"But when I looked at it on my phone," said Toni, "I spotted another familiar face."

She zoomed in on the photograph and moved it around on the screen to show a smiling figure in the front row.

"Sayer!" gasped Agatha.

"Actually," said Mulligan, "he is Lieutenant Neil Webster. Once Toni identified him, it was easy to check him out. He joined the army straight out of university and served with Bream and Dunster in Germany. He even spoke for Bream at his court martial. He was a martial arts, fitness, and survival expert — obsessed, it seems. Then a Land Rover he was driving alone in Helmand was blown up. No body was ever recovered."

"That's because there was no body!" Agatha crowed. "He's alive and well and up to no good at Morrison's!"

"We should let the police know about him," said Toni.

"All in good time. Let's find out what those three are up to with Albert Morrison first. Wizz-Wazz should be able to help us with that."

Agatha crossed to her office, picked up the phone and hit a speed-dial number.

"Roy?" she said as soon as the call was answered. "It's me."

"Agatha, *darling*," gushed Roy Silver, "long time no hear."

"We spoke just a couple of weeks ago."

"Two weeks is a lifetime in this business, darling, as you well know."

"I need you up here tonight, Roy."

"Tonight? But I couldn't possibly, Aggie. I am absolutely and totally rushed off my poor little feet. Why else would I be in the office on a Saturday?"

Agatha imagined Roy Silver sitting with his feet on his desk in the London offices of Pedman's PR, the company that had bought her own PR business. He was the only one of her former staff still with Pedman's and had taken several giant steps up the career ladder due to Agatha having handed him a treasure trove of opportunities on a plate.

"Roy," she said, "you owe me, and this is going to put you back on the national stage again, right in the spotlight. There's been a murder."

"Another murder?" he squealed. "Do tell, darling."

By the time Agatha had finished spinning Roy Silver the tale of a sweet, adorable donkey who was to be put to death for a crime she did not commit, she had him eating out of her hand.

"I can see the headlines now," he said. " 'Donkey Framed for Murder. Wizz-Wazz Is Innocent.' I'll start rounding up the press pack and the TV and radio right now. We'll get them all at Morrison's for the first press call on Monday morning. I'll drive up to Carsely later and see you for dinner. This is going to be simply marvellous, darling!"

Agatha congratulated herself as she put down the phone. The campaign to save Wizz-Wazz was under way. It would be a cover for her to continue her investigation at the factory. Nothing at Morrison's, she smiled, was ever what it seemed.

CHAPTER SIX

Roy Silver arrived in Lilac Lane early that evening, erupting out of his small car in a blur of dusky-pink corduroy and breathless excitement. He began talking as soon as Agatha opened the front door and did not miss a beat while dumping a suitcase, rather too large even for several nights away from home, in the hall.

"I have been on the phone literally all afternoon, sweetheart. So much to tell you and something absolutely adorable to show you," he gushed. "What do you think of this look?" He struck a pose near the door. The pink corduroy trousers were matched with a flat cap, a dark brown waxed jacket, and two-tone pink-and-brown shoes. "I'm going for relaxed country fun with a hint of city sophistication," he chattered on without waiting for a response. "I'm wearing it for the press call tomorrow morning. We need to appeal across the board for the launch of

the Wizz-Wazz Is Innocent campaign —
from elderly animal-lovers to young children. The kids will draw in their parents.
You know what kids are like once they start
making a noise about something as sensitive
as a poor little donkey being put to death,
and . . ."

That, thought Agatha, as Roy continued
to talk, wasn't such a bad idea at all, and
Roy dressing himself like a caricature of a
children's TV presenter would be just right.

". . . so it's mainly regional press and
agencies with a few stringers from the
nationals for the campaign announcement
on Monday morning," he continued. "We'll
use that to generate interest and draw in the
big boys on national TV for the campaign
and product launch the following morning.
You said there was a US angle as well? We
need to capitalise on that to bring in inter-
national media and —"

"Product launch?" Agatha interrupted.
"What are you talking about?"

"Oh, just a little idea I had, darling." Roy
smiled. "I will tell you all about it over dinner. I am totally famished. Can we go to
your lovely little local pub? It's so quaint
and villagey."

Roy carried on talking all the way along
the lane and out into Carsely High Street.

160

He paused outside the Red Lion and pronounced it "adorably rural." It was, Agatha thought, walking into the bar area, really a very lovely old pub. The ceilings were low, but unlike the hideous Jolly Farmer that she had visited with Toni, the beams in the Red Lion were authentic and the atmosphere comfortably cosy. Vases of fresh flowers dotted here and there on tables brightened the large bar area. There had been a chill in the air on their walk to the pub, and she was pleased to see a log fire burning gently in the grate below the thick oak beam that served as a mantelpiece.

A few men drinking at the bar smiled and nodded, and the landlord's daughter gave them a cheery welcome as they settled at a table near the fire. She had a notepad at the ready to take their order. The menu at the Red Lion was limited, but the food was edible. They both ordered lasagne and chips. Agatha knew that the lasagne would be reheated in a microwave and would stick stubbornly to the bottom of the dish, but the chips here were always good. She asked for a bottle of white wine that she trusted. Roy placed on the table a padded brown envelope that he had brought with him.

"Is this something to do with the product?" asked Agatha.

"It is indeed," said Roy, sliding a sheet of paper out of the envelope. "Ta-daaa!"

On the sheet were a number of T-shirt designs featuring a donkey wearing something red and fluffy around its neck. Agatha couldn't recall telling Roy about the coat she had inadvertently donated to Wizz-Wazz, but she clearly must have done. Accompanying the image were slogans: *Wizz-Wazz Is Innocent!*, *Save Wizz-Wazz!* and *Don't Let Me Die!*

"Remarkable," said Agatha. "The donkey isn't quite the right colour, and the coat needs to look more furry than fluffy —"

"These are only roughs," Roy bristled, retrieving the paper, "that I had our in-house designer mock up. We'll have better by Tuesday."

"They're great," said Agatha, smiling. "I wasn't expecting T-shirt designs, that's all."

"Well you're going to love this, then," Roy replied, his enthusiasm magically restored. Reaching into the envelope once again, he gave an unconvincing imitation of a drum roll and cymbal clash, then produced with a flourish a small cloth donkey toy wearing a red fluffy collar. He stood it on the table. "This is Wizz-Wazz the Cranky Donkey!" He squeezed it and it barked like a dog. Agatha laughed.

"I have heard Wizz-Wazz make a number of different noises," she said, "but never 'Woof'!"

"It's just a prototype." Roy grinned. "The production model will go 'Hee-haw.' A contact in the soft toy business got this to me before I left the office. We can market these with profits going to the Wizz-Wazz Is Innocent campaign, or a donkey sanctuary, or whatever."

"*All* of the profits?" asked Agatha, raising an eyebrow.

"Well, clearly I will have certain . . . expenses to recoup."

"Dinner's on you, then."

"Of course," said Roy. "We can go through our plans in detail tomorrow. I'll call in a few favours and we will be ready to roll by Monday morning. Now, tell me again about the murder — and I want to hear all about the absolutely fabulous Aphrodite."

"Why the hell are there so many of them?" demanded Albert Morrison, staring out of his office window on Monday morning. Half a dozen cars filled the small parking area outside the factory, and others were bumping off the drive to park on the grass verge.

"The Raisin woman has brought in a PR man from London," said John Sayer. "He's stirred up some interest across the region."

"We don't need anyone stirring up interest in our business!" barked Morrison. He turned to face Sayer, who stood on the other side of the desk along with Farley Dunster. "Make sure they all behave themselves. We don't know who any of those press people are, so keep an eye on them. Count them in and count them out again. I don't want anyone hanging around here afterwards."

"They will be back tomorrow," said Sayer. "More of them, probably."

"Then you'll have to do the same tomorrow, won't you?" Morrison shouted at him. "I don't know why we're letting them stage this farce here."

"It would have looked odd if we hadn't," said Sayer calmly, "and your wife was —"

"Keep an eye on her too," growled Morrison. "We can't afford to let any of this affect our plans. We have a schedule to maintain. Tell the Raisin woman I want to see her as soon as she has done her bit in front of the press. Now get down there and keep this shambles under control!"

The two men turned to go.

"And Dunster," Morrison called. "Best leave your little toy with me for now."

Dunster looked at Sayer, who nodded. He

stripped off his jacket to reveal a leather holster nestling under his left arm. A dark glimmer of gunmetal caught the light as he removed the holster. He wrapped its straps around it and placed it on Morrison's desk. Morrison picked up the gun and locked it in his desk drawer.

The weather was kind to them for the press call. Agatha felt relieved. It was not something that either she or Roy could control. A few fluffy clouds crept across a weak blue sky, but there was no hint of rain. Perfect, she thought, for the photographs.

She watched Roy Silver at work, marshalling a small scrum of photographers and keeping up a stream of instructions, parrying journalists' requests and imploring them all to be patient. He certainly stood out from the crowd in his pinkness. Agatha herself had chosen a more sober look that she felt would better reflect her role as the head of a detective agency. The dark blue Max Mara trouser suit was suitably restrained. Roy would play the role of the eccentric and colourful campaign manager, while she would give serious interviews. One would entertain, the other would inform. This wasn't a "good cop, bad cop" situation, she reflected, more "clown and ringmaster."

She turned to Toni at her side. "Okay, Toni," she said softly. "All the attention is now going to be on that lot. You can slip away and try to sneak into the dispatch department. Have a good look around. If any of the regular workforce are in today, have a word with them. Ask if they've noticed anything unusual going on."

"Apart from a murder and media circus, you mean?"

Agatha shot her a look.

"Okay, I'm going."

"Mrs. Raisin!" Agatha heard John Sayer approaching. Or rather, the missing-presumed-dead Lieutenant Neil Webster. She eyed him cautiously, determined to maintain a neutral expression. She was not prepared to give him even an inkling of the questions that were racing through her mind. Why did he blow up his Land Rover? How did he get out of Afghanistan? How did he cross borders and travel halfway round the world without getting caught? How did he get back into the country? Why was he here at all? "Was that your young blonde friend I just saw you with? Is she leaving so soon?"

"I just asked her to check . . ." Agatha thought quickly, "that the press people were parking sensibly."

"I see," said Sayer. "That's a very good idea. We wouldn't want any more accidents, would we?" Somehow, thought Agatha, he managed to make that sound terribly sinister, almost a threat, despite his sickly-sweet smile. "Mr. Albert would like to see you in his office once you have finished here. I will take you up there."

"Fine by me," said Agatha. "Now if you will excuse me, we have to get started." So I have been summoned, she thought. All this must be getting right up Morrison's nose. Well, if he is getting rattled, then he may let something slip. I'm looking forward to having a chat with Albert Morrison.

Roy clapped his hands, jumping up and down to make sure that everyone could see him, and called for attention. Sayer shrank off into the background, positioning himself, Agatha noted, as though he were guarding the route from the stable yard to the factory. She looked in the other direction and saw Dunster lumber into view, lurking on the route towards the drive. We are being contained, she thought. They don't want any of us wandering around where we shouldn't.

"Now come along, everyone," Roy called, projecting his voice across the small crowd of press people. "Now that we're all here, I want to introduce you to a very special character. Ladies and gentlemen, the adorable Wizz-Wazz!"

That was Peter Trotter's cue to present the star of the show. He hauled on the donkey's harness, dragging Wizz-Wazz towards the waiting photographers and journalists. She still had the fun fur draped around her shoulders. Even now, in its dishevelled state, Agatha coveted the coat. It had been such a lovely thing to wear. Why on earth had she given it to the donkey? As soon as I get the chance, she promised herself, I am taking myself off on a shopping trip to London to find a nice new clean one just like it.

"Come on, you stinkin' swine," muttered Trotter out of the side of his mouth. Wizz-Wazz grunted and viewed the strangers in her yard with hooded eyes. She doesn't look happy, thought Agatha. Maybe I can calm her down and —

"Thass ma Wizz-Wazz, baby!" The shrill of Aphrodite Morrison was unmistakable. John Sayer led her forward and then let her loose in the stable yard. Her blonde hair tumbled in waves down to her shoulders. She wore sunglasses, a gold Puffa jacket, black leggings emblazoned with gold stars, and gold hi-top trainers. She was showered with flashes from a dozen cameras as she stepped in front of the photographers.

"Ladies and gentlemen!" called Roy, determined to recapture centre stage. "This is Wizz-wazz's devoted owner —"

"I am Aphro-nighty Norrishon," slurred Aphrodite, advancing towards Wizz-Wazz, stumbling slightly and holding out a carrot. Incredible, thought Agatha. It's barely ten thirty in the morning and she is plastered! Drunk as a skunk!

Wizz-Wazz made a grab for the carrot, and in doing so nipped one of Aphrodite's fingers.

"Yeeeoww!!" she squealed. "Shon of a bitch!" She drew back her arm and aimed a slap at the donkey, who easily dodged out of the way. Aphrodite followed through and caught Peter Trotter full in the face. Cameras whirred and flashes fired, but Roy was already on top of things, having positioned himself between Aphrodite and the photographers, effectively blocking any chance they had of capturing the moment on film.

The real photo opportunity, as Sayer stepped in to hustle Aphrodite away, came an instant later, when Wizz-Wazz sauntered past the press pack to Agatha, gently tucked her head under Agatha's arm and turned her huge brown eyes to face the cameras. It was a pose so gloriously endearing that it captivated even the most hardened cynics of the media corps, and a low chorus of "Aaah" could be heard while the cameras clicked and whirred.

Reporters clamoured for Agatha's attention as the flashes continued to burst. In front of them all stood Charlotte Clark. She grinned and mouthed, "Exclusive." Agatha nodded, and then Charlotte all but disappeared as reporters thrust arms over her head, pointing microphones and recorders in her direction. "How did you make friends with Wizz-Wazz, Agatha? Why does she love you so much?" Agatha could hear herself answering their questions as though it were someone else talking. For a moment she felt strangely detached, her mind racing, because at that instant she realised what was missing from the murder scene. No — she briefly turned to survey the stable yard — there was something else. The picture was still incomplete, but she now knew what one of the missing pieces looked like. All they had to do was find it.

Their questions exhausted, Roy Silver ushered the press people back towards their cars. "Don't forget," he said. "We will have a product launch here tomorrow at the same time, with press packs and giveaways and details of how to run competitions so that your readers can win the chance to meet Wizz-Wazz in person and . . .”

Agatha led Wizz-Wazz back to her loose box. Am I getting to like you? she wondered. I doubt you will ever be my favourite animal, but maybe . . . She stroked the donkey's head, then caught a whiff of donkey pong from her own hand . . . Maybe not.

Trotter appeared and slammed shut the loose box door. He had a red mark on the side of his face.

“You don't have much luck with women, do you, Trotter?” Agatha said.

“You better watch your mouth,” he hissed, taking a step towards her.

“Cut that out, Trotter!” John Sayer strode across the yard. Trotter spat on the ground at Agatha's feet and skulked away.

“He's such a charmer,” said Agatha to Sayer. “What rock did you find him under, Mr. Human Resources Manager?”

“Would you come with me, please? Mr. Albert is waiting for you.”

Albert Morrison looked up from a document on his desk, his face grim, when Sayer showed Agatha into his office.

"Mrs. Raisin," he said, pointing out of the window towards the stables. "I dislike having that sort of pantomime performed on my premises!"

"Good morning to you too, Mr. Morrison," said Agatha. "Your wife played something of a starring role in that pantomime, didn't she?"

"You leave my wife out of this!" shouted Morrison. "You have caused us nothing but embarrassment here, Mrs. Raisin, and I want you out. Your contract is terminated." He picked up the document on his desk and held it in front of Agatha so that she could see it was the contract they had signed, then tore it to shreds and dumped it in a pile back on the desk.

"Very dramatic," said Agatha, "but I have a copy of that contract, too."

"Then you will know," said Morrison, "that there is a clause in it forbidding you from doing anything that might bring the company name into disrepute. You are most certainly in breach of that clause. You won't be getting a penny in payment."

A side door to the office opened and Angus Bream strutted in, his hand clamped around Toni's upper arm. He shoved her roughly towards Agatha.

"She is never to be allowed on these premises again under any circumstances," Morrison declared. "You, Mrs. Raisin, will confine your activities tomorrow to the stable yard. I never want to see you again. Now get out."

Agatha gave Toni a look of concern. Toni nodded and shrugged. She was fine.

"I'm going," said Agatha, leaning across the desk, "but you have not seen the last of me, Albert Morrison." She flipped the pile of torn paper into the air and it rained down on Morrison like giant confetti. Agatha Raisin then left the building.

Agatha, Toni, and Roy sat in the King Charles pub opposite the Raisin Investigations office. They ordered sandwiches and drinks and used their lunch to review the events of the morning.

"I thought it all went exceptionally well," said Roy, "apart from the Aphrodite incident and we needn't worry too much about that. Most of the press didn't really see what happened and none of them got a photo. There will be some utterly divine shots of you with Wizz-Wazz, though, Aggie. You looked sensational together!"

"I think I managed to give them plenty about how wonderful she is." Agatha smiled. "The big question was always: if Wizz-Wazz is innocent, then who did kill Mrs. Dinwiddy?"

"You need to stick to the plan on that one, Aggie dear," said Roy. "You can't comment on an ongoing investigation. Tomorrow, once we have led them through the campaign again, you can give Raisin Investigations a big plug, talk about your track record, and say that any evidence you uncover will be handed to the proper authorities."

"Not that we really have any evidence yet," said Toni.

"Not yet," said Agatha, "but I now know what we should be looking for."

"What do you mean?" asked Toni.

"Something that was definitely missing from the murder scene," Agatha explained. "Mrs. Dinwiddy's digital recorder."

"Of course!" said Toni. "She always carried that thing on a strap around her wrist. I would have seen it when I checked her pulse. It definitely wasn't there."

"And whoever she recorded on that thing," said Agatha, "and whatever they said may well be what led to her death. I think Mrs. Dinwiddy found out something that meant she had to be silenced."

"So we have to find her recorder," said Toni. "Where do we start looking? At the

174

factory?"

"It's not going to be easy to get back in there," Agatha said. "You are completely banned and they'll never let me out of their sight. What happened to you this morning?"

"Actually, I did find a way into the factory," said Toni. "Bream kept yelling at me to tell him how I managed it. I told him that I walked in the front door, but he didn't believe me. He caught me chatting to one of the girls in the dispatch department. She told me that they are all kicked out of the place at the end of the day, but that often when they come back in the morning, it's obvious that people have been in there during the night. Then Bream grabbed me and hauled me away."

"So how *did* you get in?" Roy asked.

"The R&D building isn't secure," Toni explained. "Most of it's burnt out. The doors to the outside are hanging off. The part that is attached to the side of the main building is the least damaged, although it's still all black and charred. There's no obvious way through, but there was a door to a ladies' loo in R&D. It looked locked, but I gave it a shove and it opened. The lock and part of the door frame came away. When I closed it from the other side, it looked like it was still firmly locked. The R&D loo is linked to the ladies' loo in the main building through a door that wasn't locked, although it is now."

"How do you know it's locked now?" Agatha asked.

"Because," said Toni, reaching into her pocket, "I locked it, and here's the key."

"Very clever," said Agatha. "So anyone who even suspects you came in that way is going to find nothing but locked doors, yet we may be able to use that route again."

"That doesn't sound like a terribly good idea to me," said Roy, shaking his head. "If you were prowling around and got caught by those dreadful thugs . . ."

"It's an option," said Agatha, taking the key from Toni, "and right now we need to consider every option."

"Right now I need to use your office, Aggie," said Roy. "I have to chase up a lot of stuff for tomorrow and try to make sure that you and Wizz-Wazz make some of the evening news reports. We will definitely have the regional morning papers, and that will bring the big boys buzzing like bees around a honeypot."

As Roy made his way across the lane, Agatha was suddenly struck by what he had said. *Bees around a honeypot.* She felt a thrill of pride and excitement. That's me, she thought. I am the honeypot! After all those years in PR in London, arranging junkets and organising publicity for other people, I am now the centre of attention. The thing about Dinwiddy's recorder distracted me, but all those press people were desperate to talk to *me*. This time I am the star. Agatha Raisin is about to become a celebrity!

"See if you know where that is," she said to Toni, handing her Elizabeth Thirkettle's address. "I need to consider what I will say to my public tomorrow."

Toni drove Agatha out of Mircester, along the road towards Charlbury. The day remained fair and Agatha gazed out of the car window and beyond the hedgerows to where fields lay already ploughed, prepared for winter. Some potato crops had yet to be harvested, providing green pockets on the patchwork of rich earth that spread itself across the gently rolling hillsides. Now and again she spotted red kites wheeling gracefully in the sky, their long wings outstretched to catch every thermal and helpful gust as they patrolled the countryside.

"Sparrow Farm Lane should be next on the left," said Toni. She turned into a narrow rutted lane and the car rocked from

177

side to side, heaving itself from one wheel-carved trough to the next. Agatha felt her lunchtime sandwich threaten to reappear, but the lane thankfully smoothed itself out and they drew up outside a stone farmhouse.

"This is it," Toni announced, unclipping her seat belt. "Sparrow Farm."

The building was a large farmhouse, too big to be called a cottage and too small and plain to be deemed a manor house. An open wooden porch protected the front door, and roses stood in beds to either side, humbly offering their last fading pink flowers.

"I think I was expecting something a little more grand," Agatha sniffed. "It's not exactly palatial, is it?"

She rattled the large black lion's-head knocker and Clive Thirkettle opened the door, his curly silver locks forming a halo against the darkness of the inner hallway.

"Come in, Mrs. Raisin," he said. "We have been expecting you."

He led Agatha and Toni through to a drawing room, where Elizabeth Thirkettle sat by an ornate wooden fire surround. Light flooded in from the large windows at the front of the house, and the room was furnished with two sofas and two armchairs, a sideboard, and a display cabinet, all solid

Georgian pieces, as was the coffee table that sat in front of the fireplace. It was, Agatha decided, elegantly comfortable.

Elizabeth Thirkettle stood to shake hands with her guests. They were invited to sit, and Clive left the room, promising to bring back tea and Garibaldis.

"Thank you for coming, Mrs. Raisin," said Elizabeth. "It means a great deal to me that you are taking this whole dreadful business seriously."

"Oh, we all are," said Agatha, the image of a barking toy donkey flashing through her mind. "What I would really like is to find out more about your sister."

"That is us," said Elizabeth, pointing to a silver-framed photograph on the mantelpiece. Two young girls in summer dresses stood smiling in the sunshine. The elder one was clearly Elizabeth, the younger Clarissa. They were standing, to Agatha's astonishment, with their arms around the necks of two hairy, tall-eared grey donkeys.

"The donkeys," Elizabeth said, watching Agatha's face. "That picture was taken in the field just beyond the front door, right outside this house. There were always donkeys in that field. This is where we were brought up."

"You've lived here all your life?" Toni asked.

"Not yet." Elizabeth smiled. "In fact, when Clive and I married, we spent a great deal of time abroad. The United States, the Middle East, Burma — they call it Myanmar nowadays, don't they? Clive worked for an oil company. When Clarissa married Henry Dinwiddy, she moved to a large modern house in Hampshire. Henry started life as a builder but bought and sold property, mainly around London. He became a very wealthy man.

"When Clive retired and our parents died, we came back to this house, as did Clarissa when Henry passed away a few years ago."

"Did Clarissa have any children?" Agatha asked.

"No, she never did," said Elizabeth. "Clive and I have two sons, both grown up now and working in Singapore. They were brought up mainly in Asia, and they have stayed out there."

"So Clarissa inherited Henry's fortune?" said Toni.

"That's right," Elizabeth confirmed. "She had no money worries."

A clinking of teacups from the hall announced the imminent arrival of Clive Thirkettle. He placed the tray carefully on the coffee table and let out a sigh of relief, clearly delighted that he had managed to deliver the best china unscathed. Toni offered to pour and he gratefully relaxed into an armchair.

"If Clarissa was a wealthy woman," asked Agatha, "why was she working for Albert Morrison?"

"That is something that I will never properly understand," said Elizabeth. "She had always been very much involved with Henry's business. She was a great organiser. Very efficient. Henry needed her backing him up to keep on top of the business. I think she believed that Albert Morrison was another Henry. She met him at a village fête in Carsely. She seemed to invest all of the affection that she once had for Henry in a new relationship with Morrison — transferred all her love to him. She adored him and couldn't see, as we could, that he was not a very nice man."

"Absolute scoundrel," muttered Clive. "A little warm in here, isn't it, dear?"

"Not now, Clive," said Elizabeth. "Clarissa was devastated when he married that Aphrodite woman, but she was convinced it was a marriage of convenience."

"What do you mean?" Agatha asked.

"The woman had become an American

citizen," said Clive. "No longer had a British passport. He told her that if she married him, she would be allowed to stay in this country. It is really very hot, I'm afraid, Elizabeth . . ."

"Oh, go on then," said his wife.

Agatha looked at Clive in alarm as he unbuttoned his cardigan. How far was he going? What was it his wife didn't want him to do? Was he some kind of nudist? Then he reached a hand into his silver curls and pulled, revealing a glistening, completely bald head. He patted it with a handkerchief.

"I beg your pardon, ladies," he said, dropping the wig in his lap. "Elizabeth likes it, but I can't stand the thing."

"It reminds me of when we were young," said Elizabeth, then laughed when she saw Toni's wide eyes. "But maybe the time's come to give up on it."

"So Aphrodite thought she had to marry Morrison to live in the UK," said Agatha, "which probably isn't true. What did he get out of it? A trophy wife?"

"What he hoped to get," said Elizabeth, "was his hands on her money. The business was failing and he was virtually broke. She, however, made him sign a prenuptial agreement. She was prepared to give him a very generous monthly allowance, but he wasn't having her fortune. Even if she were suddenly to die, he wouldn't get it. Under those circumstances, it would all go to an animal charity. He was greedy or desperate enough to accept that, doubtless in the hope that the money would one day somehow be his."

"In the meantime, however," said Agatha, "the business was still in trouble. Did he ask for money from Clarissa?"

"Repeatedly," Elizabeth said, "but she wouldn't give him a penny. She wanted him to leave Aphrodite, give up the business and set up home with her — but she would remain in control of the purse strings. So there he was, with two wealthy women, neither of whom were prepared to bail him out."

"And then there was Josie," said Toni. "Do you know about her?"

"Clarissa told us all about her." Elizabeth sighed. "It was Clarissa who gave her the money to go off on her travels. Aphrodite was one thing, but that strumpet was quite another."

"And Clarissa liked donkeys?" asked Agatha, returning to the photograph.

"She loved donkeys," said Elizabeth. "She was besotted with Wizz-Wazz, and the feeling was mutual. I think Aphrodite only kept Wizz-Wazz because it annoyed Morrison, reminded him that there was an animal charity waiting for her millions should anything happen to her. The only person who showed the creature any love was Clarissa, which always amazed everyone given how prickly she could be with people at the factory. Wizz-Wazz returned that affection. That is why I know, Mrs. Raisin, that there was no way that donkey could possibly have killed my sister."

"We've been looking for something that belonged to Clarissa," said Agatha. "A recording device. She always carried it with her."

"Mr. Sayer from the factory brought a box of her things," said Elizabeth. She led the way to a door at the far side of the room. "It's in here, in the study."

Agatha and Toni followed her, and Elizabeth showed them a small cardboard box sitting on a writing desk. In it were a scarf, a pair of gloves, a fountain pen, a case for spectacles and, right at the bottom, the recording device. Agatha picked it up and handed it straight to Toni, grinning in triumph.

"How does it work?" she asked, displaying her customary grasp of technical gadgetry.

"You switch it on like this," said Toni, pressing the power button, "and the display will show you the files stored on it." Then her face fell. "Except there's nothing on it."

"But this was what Clarissa used to record people," Agatha sighed. "It should be full of bits and pieces of conversations. Sayer must have wiped it clean before returning it with her other things!"

"It might actually have been full," said Toni, twiddling the machine in her fingers as she thought. "A device like this won't carry on recording forever, but I don't think Clarissa would want to delete her recordings. If I was her, I would want to *transfer* them to another device to store them, leaving this one empty to carry on recording. Mrs. Thirkettle, did Clarissa have a computer or a laptop?"

"That's what Sayer asked when he brought back her things," said Elizabeth. "He said he needed to be sure that there were no company documents being kept outside of the factory. I told him she didn't have any kind of computer here."

"Shit!" said Agatha, making no attempt to hide her disappointment, then, "Sorry!" when Elizabeth raised an eyebrow.

"Well, I agree that it would have been fairly shitty," said Elizabeth. "But I didn't trust that man Sayer. So I lied." She unlocked a drawer in the desk and produced a slim silver laptop computer. Toni opened it, pressed the power button and waited. The screen flickered into life, showing a photograph of Clarissa Dinwiddy standing proudly at Albert Morrison's side. They were clearly at some kind of official function, as both were dressed in evening wear.

"We need her password," said Toni.

"I'm afraid I wouldn't know that," said Elizabeth. "I have never taken much of an interest in that sort of thing."

Agatha glanced back at Mr. Thirkettle, who was now lolling in his armchair, head back, eyes closed, and mouth open — sound asleep. His silver wig sat in his lap like a bizarre codpiece, yet looking like it might hop down onto the floor and make a break for the door at any moment.

"And neither has he," said Mrs. Thirkettle, tutting at her husband and shaking her head when she realised he had nodded off.

"Maybe we can guess it," said Agatha, returning to peer over Toni's shoulder. "Most people use something that's easy for them to remember, don't they? I always use —"

"1-2-3-4-5," said Toni.

"How did you know that?"

"I've had to find things on your computer lots of times when you've been out of the office." Toni laughed. "You don't have much patience with these things, so that was the obvious combination to try, and it worked first time."

"Really?" said Agatha. "Obvious?" I will change that first chance I get, she thought. I'll make it "Hodge Boswell." That should be easy enough to remember.

"The other thing that lots of people do," Toni continued, "is to use the names of their pets."

Blast! Agatha thought. Maybe I'll make it "Charles."

Toni's fingers flashed across the keys. "No," she said, "It's not Wizz-Wazz. Another common thing is to use the name of a loved one."

Oh for goodness' sake! Agatha sighed.

"Are you okay?" Toni asked, looking up from the keyboard.

"Yes, yes!" Agatha snapped. "Look at that photograph of them together. Try Albert."

"It's not Albert," said Toni, having typed in the name. "How did she refer to him, though? 'Mr. Albert' was what she said, wasn't it? No, it's not that either. I'll try Albert M. No, no luck there. Hang on a minute, though . . ."

She plucked her phone out of her pocket and her thumbs flicked across its face, tapping in words so quickly that Agatha gave up trying to see what she was typing. Toni's thumbs reminded her of the flippers on a pinball machine. Agatha had played pinball only once, many years ago, trying to impress a young man who, it transpired, was far more interested in the dings, toots, and flashing lights of the machine than he was in her. He had lost his game when she accidentally ground her heel into the top of his foot when she walked out.

"What are you doing?" she asked.

"Internet . . . anagram," said Toni, returning to the laptop keyboard. "That's it!" she whooped. "We've got it. Mrs. Dinwiddy's password was Mr. Table, an anagram of Albert M."

The computer screen changed to show a host of little icons.

"That's a lot of folders," said Toni, choosing one and clicking on it. "And inside there are yet more folders."

"Get on with it," said Agatha impatiently. "What's in them?"

"Bingo," said Toni. "Sound files. This is where she dumped her recordings. There must be thousands of them. Hours upon hours of the stuff."

"Mrs. Thirkettle," said Agatha, crossing back into the sitting room with Elizabeth.

Mr. Thirkettle's wig had migrated to his knee. She wondered if he had woken and moved it, or if it had crawled there itself. "Do you think we could borrow Clarissa's old laptop? It looks like there are rather a lot of recordings on there that we need to listen to."

"If it helps you find who murdered my sister, Mrs. Raisin," said the old lady with a slight tremble to her lip, "you are most welcome."

"Toni," Agatha called, "bring the laptop with you. You've got work to do."

CHAPTER SEVEN

Back at the office in Mircester, Toni copied all the sound files onto her own computer and Agatha locked the laptop securely away at the bottom of a metal filing cabinet. Sayer couldn't possibly know that Elizabeth Thirkettle had given them the machine, but she didn't want to take the chance that he might find out and come looking for it.

"Where should I start?" asked Toni, sitting in front of a screen crowded with numbered files.

"If you can tell which are the oldest," Agatha suggested, "best start there. We have no idea what we are looking for, so we need to check everything. There could be a few words from a factory worker, or maybe the voice of someone we know that will prove to be vital. Some of it might not be relevant . . . might even be a bit dull . . ."

After half an hour of listening to file after file of factory employees gossiping about everything from the heating on the local bus to hotel toilets in Tenerife, Toni turned to Agatha with a weary look.

"You must hate being right all the time." She sighed. "This is beyond dull. Why did she record all this stuff?"

"I suppose she never knew what might come in handy for those little revenge campaigns she told us about," said Agatha. "It's not all dull, though, is it? There was the one about the woman who came home and found her husband trying on her wedding dress . . ."

"That was a good one." Toni laughed. "And so was this." She clicked on a file, and a hushed voice came from the computer saying, ". . . she found him in the shrubbery wearing nothing but odd socks and a woolly hat . . ."

"I wonder if that was the same man?" Agatha smiled, then looked at her watch. "Is that the time? I need to get home. Roy is meeting me there with the evening papers."

"I'll plough through this for a while longer," said Toni, clicking on the next file.

". . . my Jake were full of chat when we first met," came the voice of a middle-aged woman. "Now he's just full of crap . . ."

Agatha had barely had time to pour herself

a gin and tonic and flop into an armchair before Roy Silver breezed through the front door carrying an armful of newspapers.

"Success, darling!" he beamed. "We've made the evening papers across the region and the radio stations are all picking up on it too! My phone has been ringing itself to pieces and absolutely everyone is showing up for the product launch and photo call tomorrow morning!"

He unfolded a newspaper to show a photograph of Agatha and Wizz-Wazz on the front page. Agatha sat forward, sizzling with excitement. She grabbed the newspaper and studied the photograph closely, but the print quality made everything look too fuzzy, so she held it at arm's length. Her hair looked good. There were a few stray strands, but it was a breezy stable yard, not a red-carpet event, so she was prepared to accept that. Her smile was assured, confident, and strong, with a hint of a gentle touch. Yes, she was pleased with her smile, especially since the quality of printing combined with her make-up to hide any wrinkles. Oh no! Was that lipstick on her teeth? No, just bad printing again.

Mumbling "Mmmm, yes," and "Not bad at all," she compared the front-page photo with two others that Roy held up, taken from different angles. Overall, she considered her left profile the most pleasing, closely followed by the full-face shots. Wizz-Wazz, she decided, looked equally hideous from whatever angle she was photographed. Agatha was, in her own honest opinion, most definitely the star of the show.

"Hang on a minute, Roy," she said, scowling. "What's this?" She slapped the front page of one of the papers, where, alongside the photograph of her and Wizz-Wazz, the headline read: *Local Woman Calls Mayor an Ass.*

"Local rags." Roy shrugged. "They're always doing things like that. They've done a good job on the story inside, though. Another photo, too."

" 'Private investigator Agatha Raisin today launched a campaign to save Wizz-Wazz the donkey. Full story on page five.' " Agatha read out the picture caption above the sound of a knock at the front door. "See who that is, would you, Roy?" She rustled through the paper, accidentally skipping past the page she wanted to where another article caught her eye.

"Hey, Roy," she called, browsing the article. "There's a piece in here about Charles's house. The Mircester Country Sports Association is to hold a fair there and it says that he's . . . ENGAGED!!"

"Hello, Aggie." Agatha looked up to see Charles standing in her living room.

"You . . ." she gasped. "You're engaged. You never said a word. You never told me a thing."

"I wanted you to know," said Charles. "Honestly, Aggie . . ."

"It's *Agatha*," she growled, standing to face him. "You wanted me to know but you decided to tell everyone else first!" She flung the newspaper at him. "Everyone in the village must know. Everyone in the whole world knows except me! How long were you planning to keep it a secret from me? And who is she anyway? Who is this poor girl that you've hoodwinked?"

"She's really very nice," Charles said, struggling to remain calm. "From a perfectly decent family. Her name is Mary. Mary Darlinda Brown-Field. Her father runs a very successful business. Come to the country sports thing on Wednesday. She'll be there. I'd like you to meet her."

"Meet her?! You would like me to meet her, would you?!" Agatha shouted. "You want to introduce me to your latest sexual conquest? Well, I suppose that's better than simply bumping into her in your bedroom!"

"I just need to, um . . . take a look at the

thingummy . . . upstairs," said Roy, ducking out of the room. He snuck out of the front door and scurried off, heading for the Red Lion.

"I was not aware," Charles said, struggling to control a rising swell of anger, "that I was obliged to ask your permission about these things. You, after all, did not consult me about Chris Whatsisname."

"FIRKIN!"

"What?"

"Chris Firkin! That's his name!" Agatha shrieked. "I should have known that Gustav's spies would have reported back by now. And Chris is *different*. We haven't been bonking each other's brains out."

"Neither have Mary and I."

"Pardon? You haven't slept with . . ." Agatha could scarcely believe her ears. "Are you serious? That's like . . . like . . . buying a fantastic pair of shoes in London without trying them on, and then when you go to wear them to a fancy dinner in Barcelona, it turns out that they don't fit and are completely useless!"

"That actually happened, didn't it?"

"NEVER MIND!! Are you losing your touch, Charles? Or is she not interested in . . . sex?"

"She's interested. She just wants the right

time and place and —"

"After she's got her talons into you, you mean? Was this all part of some pre-nuptial non-consummation, no-nookie marriage settlement contract?"

"Actually, a marriage settlement has been agreed and —"

"Well, of course it has! Let me guess — you're going to get a whole pile of cash after the wedding but it all has to go into running the estate the way she and her daddy say. And you can't touch a penny of her inheritance and she can't promise any of it to you unless you're a very good boy for a very long time. In the meantime, you can't do so much as buy an air freshener for your BMW without their say-so!"

"That is not how it will work at all. You are being facetious and unkind. All Mary and her family want is . . ."

". . . is the kind of lifestyle they think they can *buy*, Charles. They think they're using their money to take a huge leap up the social ladder into the world of the county set. They think they can splash some cash and become part of the aristocracy. You *know* that's not the way it works. I could live in Carsely until the day I die and I will still be considered an outsider. I will never truly fit in. I will always feel like I don't

196

belong — and these are just normal villagers. You are taking money from these people and you know it will be a hundred times worse for them with your upper-crust elite than it will ever be for me here amongst ordinary people. Your new fiancée and her clan can never join that exclusive club. Your lot will always look down on them. I mean, they are in *trade,* aren't they? What is the Brown-Field family business?"

"Eminently respectable. They sell ladies' products."

"Ladies' products? What sort of products?"

"Women's things. 'Forever Yours' is one of their brands."

"They sell *sanitary towels?*"

"Well, someone has to."

"Of course someone has to, Charles, but you don't *marry* them. That's how your acquaintances are going to see it, isn't it? You don't *marry* that sort. You know what your lot are like. It's why you detest them. They will see this poor girl as a figure of fun. She may aspire to be one of them but she never will be. She is reaching for a lifestyle that she thinks you can provide, but you are sentencing her to a lifetime of misery."

"You are wrong, my dear. She is far more

aware and pragmatic than you think."

"Oh, leave me alone, Charles. I can't believe you are doing this. I thought we . . . I mean . . . Oh, just go, please."

"Very well," said Charles, turning for the door, "but we should speak again. We have been through too much together to throw it all away. You should come on Wednesday, Aggie."

"It's AGATHA!!" she screamed, snatching a cushion and hurling it at the closing door. Then she picked up another cushion, buried her face in it and wailed and sobbed until her chest ached.

"Now you are ready for this, aren't you, darling?" Roy Silver fussed around Agatha. He had a crumple of scribbled notes in one hand and a lint roller in the other, running it over Agatha's jacket to remove imagined dust specks. "We must have you looking your best. You know what you have to say, don't you? Don't try to give a big speech. When you answer questions, remember to use the slogans 'Wizz-Wazz Is Innocent' and 'Save Wizz-Wazz.'

"And don't forget those sound bites we practised. 'Even a humble donkey deserves justice' and 'I see nothing but innocence in her eyes.' You will have to lose those sunglasses, dear, and we want to see that gorgeous smile again. Eyes aren't still puffy from all that crying, are they?"

"Get stuffed, Roy."

Roy wisely decided to busy himself somewhere else, and Agatha retrieved a compact from her handbag. She flipped it open and studied herself in the mirror. Her make-up looked fine. Her hair was perfect. There was hardly a whisper of a breeze today, so she didn't have to worry about looking windblown. She took off her sunglasses. My eyes do *not* look puffy, she told herself. The early-morning ice packs took care of that. And the smile? Well, I can turn that on whenever I want.

She moved the mirror a little to the left and picked up the figure of John Sayer, positioned to keep an eye on proceedings as he had been yesterday. Glancing in the other direction, she could see Dunster in position, too. Bream would be on the main factory door, making sure that Morrison's had no unwelcome visitors. Dunster looked a little nervous. Too many people, thought Agatha. This morning's press pack had swelled in size. There were far more reporters standing around chatting, far more cars and vans cluttering the parking area and the driveway. There were even vehicles parked haphazardly wherever they could pull off the main road near the front gates. A variety of aerials and satellite dishes had been set up, and TV cameramen were hefting the tools of their trade onto their shoulders. Powerful lights blazed down on the stable yard from tall stands, while sound technicians wearing headphones and carrying huge fluffy microphones were jostling for position.

Roy, still resplendent in pink, had taken centre stage beneath the lights. He was smiling and joking with the ladies and gentlemen of the press. The warm-up act, thought Agatha. He is there preparing them for me, but I am the star of this show. They are all waiting for me. She took another look in the mirror. The same blue suit as yesterday, worn over a powder-blue silk top, also similar to yesterday's. Sticking to the same outfit was good for continuity, meaning that today's photographs would be interchangeable with yesterday's. She wanted her image to be instantly recognisable. Her audience was not yet ready for her to start experimenting with different looks.

She decided she was all set. It's show time, Agatha, she told herself. Tucking the compact back into her handbag, she began walking towards the lights, turning on her most dazzling smile.

Toni sat at her desk, a pen in her hand and a notepad open in front of her. Her other hand moved and clicked her computer mouse, opening one sound file after another. She was alone in the office. She had stayed late the night before. She had even taken some of the files home on a memory stick to carry on listening to them there. She had listened to hundreds, and there were thousands more to go. Some were snatches of conversation just a few seconds long. Others dragged on for a minute or more. She now had a system. She was sorting the files into different folders. Recordings that were clearly of no use she dropped into a folder marked "DUD." Anything that was even mildly scurrilous, she filed in a "GOOD" folder, and anything that might be evidence or even a clue, she put in her "VITAL" folder. "VITAL" was still empty.

She let out a heavy sigh and got up to make herself a cup of coffee. Listening to the recordings had been quite exciting in the beginning. She had felt a real thrill snooping on conversations — eavesdropping on people who had no idea that she was listening. But the naughtiness and novelty of hearing things not intended for her ears had soon worn off. If she had learned anything at all from the tittle-tattle on the recordings, it was that an awful lot of people led mind-numbingly dreary lives.

The recordings featured a cavalcade of complaints from men and women about their partners, their children, their jobs, and their health. The women in particular seemed to want to go into great detail about all sorts of health issues — especially other people's health issues. The whole thing was getting Toni down. Was that all she had to look forward to in getting married? Endless problems and rows over the mortgage, the kids, the house, the car, the carpets, and the curtains, and a life that descended into such monotony that backache and bunions were the most interesting things to talk about?

She stirred her coffee and decided to take a proper break. She picked up the remote control for the office TV and switched it on. Maybe there would be some kind of news bulletin from the stables. She flicked through the channels and gave a little whoop when Agatha's smiling face filled the screen.

She looks great, she thought. Maybe a bit puffy around the eyes. She turned up the volume to hear what Agatha was saying.

"... and that, ladies and gentlemen, is

what our campaign is all about — justice," Agatha's voice assured her via the TV loudspeaker. Toni watched her boss reach out to her left, a not-so-carefully-concealed carrot partially visible in her hand. Wizz-Wazz wandered into view, snatching the carrot from Agatha's hand, which she quickly withdrew, her smile fading not one flicker. "Because even a humble donkey deserves justice."

Her words were almost drowned out by the loud crunch of Wizz-Wazz chomping the carrot. Toni watched Agatha pause and look towards the donkey, still smiling sweetly. Wizz-Wazz gazed at Agatha, then turned to face the cameras, drawing every focus to the soulful dark pools of her eyes. Then she slowly batted just one long-lashed eyelid.

"Surely not," Toni said out loud, starting to giggle. "Did she just wink? Donkeys don't wink, do they?"

The press pack loved it. Toni could hear them calling, "Lovely, Wizz-Wazz!" "Look at those eyes!" "Give us another wink, Wizz-Wazz!"

Wizz-Wazz is such a star, she thought. She's really stealing the show!

In the stable yard, Agatha was beginning to

feel uncomfortably warm under the lights. Her irritation was intensified by the feeling that she might be starting to lose control of her own press call. No way, she told herself. Agatha Raisin is not about to be upstaged by a donkey! She threw her arm around Wizz-Wazz's neck and cuddled close to give a perfect photo opportunity full of affection.

"At Raisin Investigations," she said, "we are proud of our enviable reputation for rooting out injustice. Our track record in solving crime is —"

She was interrupted by a thunderous, rasping, trumpeting fart.

There was an instant of shocked silence before she attempted to continue.

"I see nothing but innocence in those —" and then she was engulfed in a stench so noxious that her throat closed up. She gagged and coughed and her eyes began to water. "SNAKES AND BASTARDS!" she screamed. "GET THIS FILTHY BLOODY ANIMAL AWAY FROM ME!"

The press pack roared with laughter. Cameras clicked and whirred, and Wizz-Wazz let out a braying "HEE-HAWW!!" accompanied by another joyous, booming, sustained parping from her rear end. Roy Silver stepped in front of Agatha, smiling, laughing, and fanning his pink corduroy cap in front of his increasingly flushed face in an effort to waft some fresh air in his direction.

"I must apologise for Mrs. Raisin," he said breathlessly.

"Really?" came a voice from the crowd. "We thought it was the donkey!"

There was even more laughter. Agatha stormed off.

Toni waited anxiously in the office. She had watched the whole debacle on TV. Agatha had gone from being a national celebrity to a national disgrace live on air. From hero to zero in the space of a donkey fart. She was not going to be happy when she arrived back at the office, and Toni was convinced that the office was where she would come. She could use her cottage as a sanctuary, but in Lilac Lane she would have to contend with friends and neighbours calling round. Here, no one could get past the street door and upstairs to the outer office if they were not welcome. And Toni knew that Agatha would rely on her to let no one past the outer office. Agatha would come here, she reasoned. She would feel safe here.

As if to confirm her theory, there came a drumming of footsteps on the stairs and

Agatha made her entrance.

"I thought that went well," said Toni. "Up to a point. You looked great on TV."

"I have warned you before about patronising me," said Agatha haughtily.

"I didn't mean to . . . I just don't know what to say."

"Then you might think about keeping your trap shut!"

"Agatha . . . look, I'm sorry. Have you thought about . . ."

". . . having a cigarette? NO, I HAVE NOT!!"

"No, have you thought about the fact that you were not to blame?"

"Well we can't blame the donkey, can we? After all, Wizz-Wazz is innocent!"

Agatha marched across the room to the rhythm of the clinking of bottles in the carrier bag she was holding. She slammed her office door. Toni sat down at her desk, leaning on her elbows, her chin in her hands.

"I thought that went well," she muttered. "What a stupid thing to say."

She was still sitting there staring at her computer screen a few moments later when she heard a voice behind her.

"Why so glum?" Agatha was back, with a glass in her hand. "It wasn't your fault either. Come and have a drink."

They sat in Agatha's office. A bottle of gin stood on the desk with a bottle of tonic keeping it company. The gin was open, the tonic was not.

"Help yourself," said Agatha. "What shall we drink to?"

"The future?" Toni suggested.

"Raisin Investigations might not have much of a future after my little outburst on national TV earlier today."

"What do you mean?"

"I mean, who's going to want to hire Agatha Raisin after that performance?"

"Can you hear yourself?" snapped Toni. Agatha's tone was starting to get on her nerves. "You sound like you've given up! 'Pull yourself together, girl!' That's what you always say to me when I'm down in the dumps. So pull yourself together! We've been in worse scrapes than this. Surely you're not going to let yourself be beaten by a flatulent donkey?"

Agatha blinked. She wasn't used to being spoken to like that by an employee.

"If we'd drunk a little more, I would have put that down to the gin doing the talking," she said, "but as things stand, you're right. We're not to blame for this, Albert Morrison is, and I'm going to get the bastard!"

"The door was wide open," said Bill

Wong, walking into the office, "so I just came straight up."

"So much for keeping people out." Toni sighed.

"Drink?" asked Agatha. "Or not while you're on duty?"

"I'm not on duty." Bill smiled. "So yes, please."

Toni decided to get back to the sound files and left Bill and Agatha alone.

"You didn't have much to say at the inquest on Saturday," said Agatha.

"It wasn't my place to say anything," said Bill, "but I wasn't happy about the way it was handled. We may be overworked and under strength, but even a straightforward accident needs proper attention. Mrs. Dinwiddy deserved better. You have to show some respect for the dead."

Those words, thought Agatha, could have come straight from your father. Agatha knew Bill's parents well. His mother was a Gloucestershire lass, but his father was Hong Kong Chinese. That mix was what gave Bill his slightly Oriental good looks. Respect for your elders. Respect for the dead. That was the Chinese way.

"I'd like to show Mrs. Dinwiddy some respect," said Agatha, "by finding her murderer."

"You are convinced it's murder," said Bill, sounding more than slightly exasperated, "but there is no evidence."

"Let me fill you in," said Agatha, and she talked Bill through everything that had happened since she gave him her statement in her cottage living room.

"I had already looked into Bream and Dunster," Bill admitted once she had finished, "and Trotter we know of old. I told you that I didn't much like some of Morrison's men. Sayer is a different kettle of fish. I will check with the military police if they would like us to collar him for them."

"Not yet," said Agatha. "If you nick Sayer, we risk never getting to the bottom of all this and finding the murderer."

"I'm not at work until tomorrow afternoon" — Bill grinned — "and we are so busy that it might take me at least another day even to contact the military, especially as it's related to a case that I have been told is closed."

"You should both hear these," said Toni, popping back into the room and beckoning them out towards her computer. "I got bored ploughing through the ancient stuff from four or five years ago and started dipping into more recent files. There's still a load of rubbish to wade through, but these are very interesting. I think Dinwiddy must have managed to make some secret recordings while she was hiding out of sight." She clicked on a file to play.

"Git rid of dat stoopid tart before I git back or I swear I'm gonna kill her, ya hear?"

"Aphrodite," said Toni. "But who was she talking about?"

"Could be Dinwiddy," said Bill, "but could also be Josie, the receptionist."

"The real question," Agatha pointed out, "is who was she talking *to*? We know she has a temper. We know she has money. Was she talking to the murderer? Did she pay to have Dinwiddy killed?"

"Or was Dinwiddy present for that recording," countered Toni. "Aphrodite could be telling *her* to get rid of Josie, which we know Dinwiddy did."

"Either is possible," said Bill. "What else do you have?"

"I hate the damn donkey and I hate her! She's on my back the whole time, tellin' me to brush it, or feed it, or muck it out!"

"Trotter," said Agatha. "I'd recognise that voice anywhere."

"Shh . . . wait," said Toni, holding a finger to her lips.

"The boss's wife likes having the donkey around and the boss likes having his wife's

money around, so for now the donkey stays . . . until we have dealt with our other problem."

"That's Sayer," said Agatha. "Could their 'other problem' have been Dinwiddy?"

"And who was Trotter talking about?" asked Bill. "Dinwiddy or Aphrodite?"

"Dinwiddy, I'd say," Agatha decided. "Aphrodite doesn't really care about Wizz-Wazz. She wouldn't hassle Trotter about looking after her."

"But something weird is definitely going on," said Toni. "Listen to this . . ."

"The first consignment is due tomorrow night. We need everybody here to deal with it."

"Morrison!" said Agatha. "But what does he mean by 'consignment'?"

"They bring in consignments of batteries," said Toni. "I saw them unpacking them and repacking them into small orders for dispatch before Bream captured me."

"But that was during the day," Agatha pointed out. "The workforce isn't there at night."

"And 'consignment' or 'shipment,' " Toni pointed out, "are the sort of words that the Mafia use when they're talking about *drugs*!"

Bill looked at her and raised his eyebrows.

"What?" said Toni, shrugging her shoulders. "I've seen it on TV."

"It certainly all sounds suspicious," Bill said, "but none of it is real evidence. It wouldn't stand up in court. Any good defence lawyer would tear it to shreds. The recordings themselves are probably illegal."

"Killjoy," said Agatha.

"I think they give us something to think about," said Toni.

"They do," Agatha agreed. "Keep on it, Toni, and forget about the old stuff. Start working backwards from the newest ones. I'm going to head home. I want to shower and change. This suit feels like it's going rigid with donkey fart."

"It feels like what?" said Bill, laughing.

"Er . . . you haven't seen the TV news?" Toni asked.

"You're in for a treat," said Agatha.

Agatha parked by her front gate and stepped out onto the pavement just as Roy Silver drew in behind her car.

"Aggie, sweetie," he twittered. "I am so glad I caught you. This whole day has just gone absolutely haywire. I have to pack, darling. I need to get back to London straightaway."

"I understand, Roy," Agatha said. "If I

were you, I wouldn't want to be seen associating with me either."

"What are you talking about?" said Roy, trotting up the garden path at her side. "You mean this morning? Oh, everyone's forgotten about that already, darling. You know what this business is like. We have to move fast. We have to move on, move forward to the next big thing. And the next big thing, Aggie, is Wizz-Wazz. The whole country has gone crazy for Wizz-Wazz the Cranky Donkey! My contact in the toy business is already working on a donkey prototype that not only goes 'Hee-haw!' but also winks and farts. How fabulous is that?"

That, thought Agatha, is a glowing cloud of fabulousness on which I really do not want to be floating. She chatted to Roy while he stuffed clothes and toiletries into his giant suitcase, then waved him goodbye as he trotted down the path to his car.

Once Agatha had freshened up, she picked out the most colourful sweater she could find and matched it with a loose-fitting pair of casual cream trousers. More loose-fitting than I expected, she thought, tugging at the waistband with her thumbs. Then she realised that she hadn't eaten a thing all day.

Hodge and Boswell ambushed her as soon

213

as she walked into the kitchen. She stroked them playfully and set food in their bowls. The microwave stood patiently waiting, but she could find nothing to tempt her amongst her stock of frozen ready meals. She decided to take a walk to catch some fresh air while the day still held some light.

A few minutes later, she was strolling past the church and the vicarage. Margaret Bloxby was raking an early fall of leaves in the garden.

"Hello, Agatha," she called. "I saw you on the news earlier. You looked very glamorous on TV."

"Kind of you to say so," said Agatha, "but I don't think it was exactly my finest hour."

"I shudder to think," said the vicar's wife, "what I would have said if I had been in your shoes. Would you like to come in for a sherry? That's not what I would have said, I mean . . ."

"I'd love to," said Agatha.

"It's Mrs. Raisin, Alf," Mrs. Bloxby called to her husband, pulling off her gardening gloves and making her way up the hall. Agatha could see Alf Bloxby scribbling at a pad of paper in his study. "He's working, as usual." Mrs. Bloxby smiled at her. "We'll be in the drawing room, Alf!"

"I suppose everyone will have seen the TV

thing by now," said Agatha as they clinked glasses, comfortably ensconced in armchairs by the window.

"Probably," agreed Mrs. Bloxby, "but it will soon be forgotten. Surely you don't regret having launched the campaign to save the donkey?"

"No, I don't regret that," Agatha admitted. "I don't have any regrets. Well, maybe a couple."

"Such as Sir Charles Fraith?"

"Perhaps," said Agatha. "You know he has become engaged? I was so angry with him for not telling me. So angry because . . ."

"Because it wasn't you?"

"I don't think that would ever have worked for us. I don't want to think about it. I have to try to move forward."

"We have no choice but to move forward," said Mrs. Bloxby. "That is how life works. We must live our lives looking forward, but we can only truly know ourselves by looking back. We are defined by everything that we have done in the past, but our only hope of change lies in the future."

"That is very . . . profound," said Agatha. "Is it part of one of Alf's sermons?"

"Not yet," said Mrs. Bloxby, craning her neck to try to see through into her husband's study, "but if he overheard it, it will be by Sunday!"

They both laughed, clinked glasses, and sipped their sherry.

"Are you still convinced that poor Mrs. Dinwiddy was murdered?" asked Mrs. Bloxby.

"More than ever," Agatha replied. "Proving it is not going to be easy, but I am determined not to give up."

"When have you ever given up? That's not what you do, Agatha. You don't give up, and you shouldn't give up on Sir Charles, either. You still have roles to play in each other's lives. Anyone can see that you two are special to one another."

"Anyone except us, it would seem," Agatha said.

They chatted until Agatha felt it was time to leave, and then she made her way back along the high street to Lilac Lane. Two local boys whizzed past on their bicycles, yelling "Hee-haw! Hee-haw!" Agatha blew them the loudest raspberry she could muster.

Tomorrow, she thought, I will put murder on hold for a morning. I will go to the country sports bash at Charles's house and face up to the future.

CHAPTER EIGHT

What did one wear to a country sports association fair? It would be mostly outdoors, so Agatha guessed that lots of people would dress for inclement weather. Waterproofs? She shuddered at the thought of an anorak. Did she even own such a thing? Maybe she had bought one on a wet day in a moment of weakness. She made a mental note to check when she had the time, and if she found one, to take it straight to the nearest charity shop.

The weather was fair but cool, so she picked out a tweed skirt, matching it with a cashmere sweater and a russet-and-gold patterned silk pashmina scarf. Then she considered gravity. Sir Thingummy Newton, she mused, may have claimed to have discovered it, but women of a certain age had certainly known about it years before when they realised that everything was heading for the floor. High heels were the answer for Agatha. They gave her the lift and shape she wanted in her calves, thighs, and bottom, but heels were a nightmare for walking on grass, which she would certainly have to do at the fair. She chose shoes with wedge heels — high enough to defy gravity but never in danger of sinking into soft turf. She took a look in the mirror. Colourful and sophisticated, with a country flavour — just right. To hell with that damned donkey. Agatha Raisin was ready to take on the world again.

Approaching Barfield House, it was clear that some sort of event was in progress. The trees and sweeping lawns that formed the park surrounding the house were normally a haven of tranquillity. Nothing disturbed the peace here. Nothing moved save for the birds, a few excitable squirrels, and the occasional deer. Today, however, there were white marquees, smaller tents with awnings, and colourful stalls arranged on one side of the driveway, and an area roped off for car parking on the other. A steward in a high-vis jacket directed Agatha into the car park, where another pointed to the space where she should leave her car.

She strolled towards the canvas village that had blossomed on the other side of the drive. She had seen events like this at Barfield before. Charles had always said that though he owned the house and the estate, it all actually belonged to the tenant farmers and the villagers — the local community. Hosting fêtes, charity events, and fairs like the one that was happening today were part of the burden of maintaining the place. The fact that most of those things also generated a bit of cash was an added bonus. That, Agatha knew, was what Charles's engagement was all about. It was neither a match made in heaven nor a union of soulmates; it was a business transaction. Charles, always struggling for money, was clearly deep in the financial mire once again.

The first tented stall she came to was selling hideously overpriced Wellington boots and outrageously expensive waxed jackets — anoraks masquerading as country fashion. Whoever thought that an anorak could have any style or allure?

"Anything I can get you?" asked the perky young man on the stall with a practised smile.

"A flame-thrower, maybe," said Agatha and walked on.

In the centre of the collection of tents and marquees was an area that had been turned into an arena, where posters announced that there would be displays by gundogs, sheepdogs, and performing ponies. Crossing this open area also gave the best view of Barfield House.

The kindest thing you could say about Barfield House was that it was big. That had never been of any great concern to Charles, except when it came to the horrendous expense of repairing and maintaining bits of the building that he scarcely remembered were even there. Agatha wondered how many times she had heard the phrase "size doesn't matter." It was a small man's mantra. To the Brown-Fields, she had no doubt, size would definitely matter. She imagined that Mary Darlinda Brown-Field's father would drive a large car, drink large whiskies, and smoke large cigars. He would have a large villa near Marbella with a large swimming pool and he would make sure that his wife wore large jewels.

Oh yes, she mused. I know the type. Large means success. Large means you have made it. Conspicuous consumption was what they called it, wasn't it? Spend lots of money on things that everyone can see cost lots of money so that the whole world knows you're a big shot. Well, Barfield House would suit them down to the ground. It was an ugly building with lots of mullioned windows. Agatha had tried to count them all once but had become bored with that very quickly. It had been built in a kind of fake-medieval style at a time when wealthy landowners were moving entire villages in order to landscape the countryside and create perfect vistas that Mother Nature had somehow neglected to provide. Tasteful it was not, but the house could be seen from a great distance. That would suit the Brown-Fields down to the ground.

Agatha was surprised by the number of people milling around. The fair had attracted a lot of visitors, and judging by the fancy motors in the car park, they were the sort of people with plenty of money to spend. She gave a start when she heard the sudden crack of gunfire.

"Clay pigeon shooting, my dear," said a man with an unfeasibly large moustache. He was standing in front of a tent displaying the wares of a company that sold and serviced shotguns. "Down by the copse. Would you like to give it a try? I think my gun would be a good fit for you, if you know what I mean?" He raised an eyebrow suggestively. That side of his moustache followed suit, as though attached by an invisible thread. Agatha gave him a look that was pure scorn and said: "Drop dead."

"Hello, fancy meeting you here!" came a

voice from behind her. Agatha recognised it straight away.

"Chris!" she said, turning to face him. "I didn't realise that you would be here."

"Nor I you." He grinned. "I was sort of obliged to take a stand to show the world what I'm up to as one of Sir Charles's tenants. Come and take a look."

Agatha slipped her arm into his and they walked together to the far side of the arena. She spotted the gleaming red camper van straight away. It looked even more highly polished, but had clearly arrived at the fair on a trailer, which was parked to one side.

"Still no engine?" asked Agatha.

"There's no fooling a detective like you, is there?" He laughed. "The wiring is pretty much in place but I haven't had time to finish that one off yet. Take a look at this, though."

On the other side of the camper was parked the old Beetle in which Chris had taken Agatha for lunch. Now, however, the dull grey paint was a deep, lustrous blue and the chrome trim glinted in the morning sunshine.

"It looks very pretty," Agatha said, admiring the cream leather interior. "It's really lovely, Chris." She wasn't quite sure how to compliment a man on how his car looked.

Motors weren't something to which she usually paid much attention. A whole row of truck-like vehicles were parked in front of the next stand. "Your little electric car is far prettier than any of those," she added, nodding at them.

"Not everyone would agree," said Chris. "Those are Land Rovers. The modern ones are more attractive, but most are built to be rugged and reliable rather than for good looks. They are the workhorses of farmers and the military."

"I met someone recently," Agatha said, "who was driving a Land Rover that was blown to bits in Afghanistan."

"Was he badly hurt?"

"Not a scratch on him as far as I know."

"Then he's a very lucky lad. Most of the Land Rovers used in Afghanistan didn't have the sort of armour that could protect anyone in them from a major explosion."

"Were you in Afghanistan?"

"I worked in submarines." He shrugged. "Afghanistan is a land-locked country. It has no seaports, so we wouldn't have been of much use there, unless we'd been tasked to launch missile strikes. I have a lot of friends in the Royal Marines, though, and they had some tough work to do on the ground in Helmand Province."

"Helmand?" said Agatha. "What were they doing there?"

"Trying to bring the Taliban, local war-lords, and drug barons under control. The drugs trade was the worst. There are huge amounts of money involved and massive areas of the countryside given over to grow-ing opium poppies to produce heroin. My friend said he had never seen so many pop-pies. He reckoned there were two hundred and fifty thousand acres of poppy fields in Helmand."

"That sounds a lot," Agatha admitted, "but to be honest, I have no idea what that means."

"Neither did I." Chris laughed. "I didn't realise how big an area that was until I came here and Sir Charles explained that his entire estate — which seems huge to me — is only one thousand acres. The heroin trade in Afghanistan is worth billions of pounds."

"Thank you, Chris," said Agatha, turning the facts over in her mind. "That's . . . interesting."

"It's not a very romantic topic of conver-sation."

"I'm a private investigator." Agatha smiled. "Information is my business."

"Well, I promise more interesting conver-sation when we go to dinner on Friday. We are still going to dinner, aren't we?"

"Definitely!" said Agatha. "I'm holding you to that — and the promise of something more interesting!"

An announcement boomed out over the public address system.

"Ladies and gentlemen! The official opening of today's events is about to take place in the main marquee. Miss Mary Darlinda Brown-Field will say a few words of welcome."

"Ooh, I don't want to miss that," said Agatha. She set off for the main marquee alone, Chris having made his apologies when a potential customer began running an admiring eye over the Beetle.

Inside the marquee, a small podium had been set up opposite the entrance. Agatha glanced to the left and right as she walked in. A preponderance of gentlemen in blazers or tweed jackets and ladies in hats confirmed that the county set was in attendance. She recognised some of the faces — minor gentry and lesser-known members of the aristocracy who, despite their relative anonymity, owned huge swathes of rural England. So, she thought, they have turned out in force to see this poor girl put on display for the first time. I almost pity her. They are all just waiting for her to fall flat on her face.

She spotted Charles to one side of the podium. He was talking to a man about his own age with thinning black hair, a very prominent jutting jaw, and eyes that were just a little too far apart. Beside him was a pretty, very neat woman with dark bobbed hair. Those, Agatha decided, must be the Brown-Fields, father and mother of the bride-to-be, and there, next to her mother, was Mary. How sad for you, thought Agatha, that you take after your father rather than your mother. Your clothes are just fine — white jacket with black velvet trim and black trousers. French tailoring. You've been shopping in Paris on the Rue Saint-Honoré, if I'm not mistaken. Very chic. But that chin and those eyes — you're definitely Daddy's girl, aren't you?

She watched Charles run a hand through his hair while Mr. Brown-Field leaned in to speak quietly to him. She knew that the hand in the hair was a sign of exasperation. Charles did not seem happy at all. Then he stepped onto the podium to stand in front of the microphone.

"Ladies and gentlemen, I would like to thank you all for coming today and, without further ado, to introduce the future Lady

Fraith, my fiancée, Mary Darlinda Brown-Field."

There was a half-hearted stutter of applause, Charles stepped away from the microphone and Mary faced the audience. She held a couple of sheets of paper in one hand and adjusted the microphone with the other.

"Thank you," she smiled, "and thank *you*, Charles. I am so happy to welcome you all here today to what in the very near future will be my home. I feel privileged that . . ." The papers slipped from her hand. "Ooh MA GAWD . . . !"

In the blink of an eye, the accent that had been practised for so long at one of England's finest ladies' colleges and perfected at one of Switzerland's most exclusive finishing schools vanished completely. The Kensington cloud parted to let London's East End come shining through. It was almost like, thought Agatha, Aphrodite Morrison losing her mystique when she spoke. Nerves had allowed Mary to drop her guard for a second. The big difference between Aphrodite and Mary was that when Aphrodite stopped speaking, she was beautiful. A few giggles in the audience were covered by light coughs, but Agatha could still hear the murmurs.

"Too much for her, I fear."

"Not really up to it."

"Well, what can you expect?"

And:

"Isn't that the donkey lady?"

Mary pulled herself together, smiled at her audience, and apologised for the slight hiatus, her cut-glass accent restored to imitation crystal perfection. A lesser girl, thought Agatha, might have let that little slip upset her, but there was no trace of a tear in those widely spaced eyes, no faltering or stuttering, just a professional smile and a smooth performance. There might be more to Mary than anyone here realised.

There was another polite, more sustained round of applause when she finished her address by wishing that everyone enjoy themselves and name-checking a few of the day's major sponsors. Her parents' products, Agatha noted, were not mentioned. Charles caught Agatha's eye, waved and made his way over with Mary by his side. Agatha braced herself and fixed a smile on her face.

"I'm very glad you came," said Charles. "Mary, I must introduce you to —"

"Mrs. Raisin." Mary smiled. "I'm so happy to meet you at last. I have heard *so* much about you."

"Really." Agatha forced a small laugh. "Charles, I do hope you haven't been giving away all our little secrets."

"No, I don't —"

"Oh, he has no secrets from me, Mrs. Raisin, do you, Charlie?"

"I am happy that —"

"I'm sure he doesn't, Miss Brown-Field. Charles has always been one to look a girl straight in the eye."

Mary's smile flickered but remained in place.

"I simply must have a proper chat with you, Mrs. Raisin. Why don't we go for a coffee tomorrow morning? There's a delightful place in the high street, not far from your little cottage, isn't there? Carsely is such a quaint village. Shall we say ten o'clock? I'll meet you there. I must go now; there are so many *important* people to talk to."

"She appears to know rather a lot about where I live." Agatha frowned as Mary strutted off into the crowd.

"She knows rather a lot about lots of things." Charles sighed.

"Not quite what I was expecting, but you are full of surprises, aren't you, *Charlie*?"

"Sir Charles," Gustav, who liked to think of himself as Charles's butler but who was actually more of a domestic manager crossed with general handyman at Barfield House, marched towards them. "Ah," he said, his black eyes darting towards Agatha, "it's you."

"What is it, Gustav?" Charles sounded irritable.

"The bloody editor of that fishing magazine," said Gustav, "is holding court in the drawing room."

"But the house is out of bounds," said Charles.

"I told him that and asked him to leave. He refused. So I flung the bastard out and told him to bugger off. Now he's demanding to see you and ranting and raving by the front door. It was all I could do to stop myself from giving him a bit of a slap."

"I'd better go," said Charles, turning to Agatha, "but I really need to talk to you. Can I take you to dinner tonight? Meet me at that French place in Broadway. You remember it?"

"I remember it," said Agatha. "See you later, *Charlie* . . ."

Charles tutted, shook his head, and ran his fingers through his hair again. Agatha decided that she had had enough of country sports for one day and headed for the car park. A small sports car had managed to become bogged down in a patch of mud.

Some men were hitching a tow rope to the front of it and preparing to pull it out using a Land Rover caked with mud. One of the men saw her watching and laughed.

"Hey, missus!" he yelled. "We'd have been able to drag this thing out of here easy as pie if you'd brought your donkey!"

"Screw you!" Agatha snarled.

She walked past, then stopped. She looked back. It was as if someone had switched on a light in her head. Of course! How could she have been so stupid? She grabbed her mobile phone from her handbag and punched in a number.

"Toni? Get Patrick back to the office now. I'll be there as soon as I can. I know who murdered Mrs. Dinwiddy!"

Patrick Mulligan was waiting by Toni's desk when Agatha stormed into the office.

"Can you find a map of the world that shows us the Middle East and Europe, Toni?" she said, perching on the edge of the desk.

Tony tapped a few keys and a world map came up on her screen. She zoomed in, putting the Black Sea and the Caspian Sea roughly in the middle of the screen.

"Let's think this through using all we have found out," said Agatha, "concentrating for the moment on Dunster, Bream, and Sayer, or Webster as we now know him to be. They have known each other for quite a few years."

"Since they served together in Germany at least," said Mulligan.

"Where there was the scandal of the stolen supplies. Let's assume that they were involved in that scam. What would they have done with the stuff they stole?"

"The easiest place to sell it," said Mulligan, "would be in Eastern Europe. Even during the Cold War, when we were facing up to the Soviets all across Germany, there were thefts from British and American supplies with the goods finding their way east. The Iron Curtain wasn't always as impenetrable as it sounds. Nowadays, if you know the right border crossing points, it must be even easier."

"So Dunster, Bream, and Sayer could have sold stuff in Eastern Europe," said Toni. "How does that help us?"

"If they were selling stolen goods," Agatha explained, "it means they developed criminal contacts in Eastern Europe — people they could rely on to sell and transport stuff. Now let's look at Afghanistan on the map, because that's where they were next posted."

"It's a big country," said Toni.

"It is more than two and a half times the size of the UK," said Agatha.

"I didn't know you were hot on geography," said Toni.

"I used the interwebby thing that you showed me," Agatha replied, "and I found out this morning that the drugs business in Afghanistan, especially in Helmand Province, is massive."

"That's certainly true," said Mulligan. "Most of the heroin coming into the UK comes from Afghanistan."

"Bream and Sayer both went missing in Helmand," Agatha pointed out. "Bream temporarily, Sayer permanently — until he turned up back here. What if they were making the same sort of contacts in Afghanistan that they did in Eastern Europe? What if they were talking to the drug barons and warlords in Afghanistan, trying to do business with them?"

"That would be a really risky business," said Toni. "The Afghan criminals would surely have seen British soldiers as spies. They wouldn't trust them. They'd be more likely to kill them."

"Risky all right," said Mulligan, "but the money to be made could make it attractive. What would they have to offer the Afghans?"

"Their contacts in Eastern Europe, perhaps," said Toni.

"Maybe," said Agatha. "How does heroin find its way from Afghanistan, where there are no seaports, to the UK?"

"My understanding," said Mulligan, "from the briefings we used to have when I was still on the force, is that the whole area is criss-crossed with camel trails that were ancient trade routes between Europe and the Far East." He pointed to the map. "The most direct route is across Iran and into Turkey, which gives you access to the Mediterranean and Eastern Europe."

"And Eastern Europe," said Agatha, "is where our gang could use their network of contacts to distribute the stuff or ship it on towards the UK. That would be useful to the drug barons. Every time the police uncover one network and shut it down, they must have to find another way to get their goods across Europe."

"That all kind of fits," Toni agreed. "When Bream and Dunster were sacked from their jobs in the warehouse in Leicester, it was for running some sort of mail order business."

"If that was to do with drugs, it could only have been small-scale," said Mulligan. "They didn't actually have control of the warehouse. Dealing with large shipments would have attracted attention."

"They obviously attracted too much attention anyway," Agatha pointed out. "They were found out and sacked. Clearly no one knew exactly what it was they were supplying by mail order."

"But at Morrison's, they do have control of the warehouse," said Toni. "Certainly at night, when the regular workforce has been cleared off the premises. And they have a facility in Sekiliv to take delivery of shipments coming in from Afghanistan."

"Exactly," said Agatha, "and a regular delivery service from the Sekiliv factory right to our doorstep here."

"But they would have to bring the drugs in through a UK port," said Toni. "They have electronic checks and sniffer dogs and things to find drugs, don't they?"

"There are lots of chemicals used in batteries," Mulligan pointed out. "That could mask any scent. They might be packing the drugs in fake batteries that are shipped in along with the real ones."

"But how did Albert Morrison get involved?" Toni asked.

"I haven't quite figured that out yet," said Agatha, "but we do know that he was desperate for money to prop up his business. The drugs operation would bring him lots of money."

"So who killed Mrs. Dinwiddy?" Toni asked.

"That," said Agatha, "is the easiest piece of the puzzle to place once you realise the two things that were missing from the murder scene. Dinwiddy's recorder was not with her body . . . and Trotter's muddy old Land Rover was not in the stable yard. He didn't walk into Mircester to visit the betting shop; he drove! He must have made sure that he was seen arriving on foot. Then he placed his bets and left on foot, but he had the Land Rover hidden nearby and drove back to the stables. Doing the journey more quickly meant that he had enough time to clobber Dinwiddy, make himself scarce, and then show up as though he had walked all the way from Mircester. I bet he had the hoof ashtray with him in his car."

"We must very nearly have caught him in the act," said Toni.

"My guess is that he heard us coming," said Agatha. "After he had whacked her, he just had time to grab the recorder and scarper before we arrived."

"So it was Mrs. Dinwiddy he was getting so angry about on the recording," said Toni, "and he was talking to Sayer!"

"The others are involved, without a doubt," said Agatha, "but it was Trotter who did the deed. He was the only one not at the party — apart from Dinwiddy. He is the murderer."

"It's a great theory," said Mulligan, "but you know what Bill Wong will say . . ."

"Yes, I know," Agatha admitted. "We have no proof. Still, it's worth mentioning to him. I'll give him a call later. Right now, however," she added, nodding at Toni, "our best chance of finding proof is definitely in those sound files. Mrs. Dinwiddy was killed because she found out what was going on, and the evidence for that is in the recordings somewhere."

"I'll get back to it," said Toni. "There are still hundreds to plough through."

"Since I'm here," said Mulligan, "I can give you a hand for a while before I have to get back to the hotel. We can transfer some files to another machine."

"No, Patrick, I need you to stay on the hotel job," said Agatha. "Morrison is never going to pay us, so we need to collect our fees on our other cases. Maybe I could help you?"

"I . . . don't think so," said Mulligan. "I don't want to blow my cover now."

"What do you mean?" Agatha asked.

"You've been the talk of the hotel," Mulligan explained. "Everyone saw you on the news. You're 'the donkey detective' or 'the donkey lady.' Everyone knows who you are."

Agatha's face fell.

"The donkey lady — that's what they're calling me? Will I ever be rid of that bloody creature?"

"Give it time, Agatha," said Toni. "It's already yesterday's news. By next week people will have forgotten all about it."

"Until the toy range comes out," Agatha muttered, stomping into her office, "or the stupid stinking animal gets its own TV series!"

The door slammed.

Agatha parked her car near the Swan pub at one end of the high street in Broadway. She threw a shawl over her head and wrapped it over one shoulder as she walked past the tables outside the pub. It was now almost dark, and too chilly to sit outside. Inside it looked comfortable and cosy, and she could see people tucking into hearty meals. No one looked in her direction. She was glad about that. She did not want to be recognised as the donkey lady.

Why is it bothering me so much? she wondered. I was sure I had moved on.

Maybe it's because no one else seems to have moved on yet, or maybe it's because of the whole situation with Charles. She cursed under her breath. The donkey should not be affecting her so much. Charles should not be affecting her so much. She hated not being in control. She hated being the donkey lady. The scarf would hide her face well enough to make it difficult for anyone to spot her. She had thought about wearing sunglasses, but sunglasses at night? Really? Only people who actually wanted to attract attention wore sunglasses at night.

Feeling like a spy or some kind of secret agent, she hurried furtively past the bow windows of closed shops and empty tea rooms. The well-lit windows of the restaurants promised warm welcomes for Broadway diners, but she resisted the temptation to peer inside. She avoided any sort of eye contact with fellow pedestrians. Before reaching the Lygon Arms Hotel, she turned off into a side street where a discreet little restaurant bathed in the glow of a street light. It served French cuisine, not so fancy or pretentious as to leave you hungry at the end of the meal, but not so robust as to be pure peasant food. She and Charles had dined there several times in the past. She could not recall Charles ever having paid, but she was determined that he would do so this evening.

Once inside, she was pleased to see that the restaurant was as dimly lit as she remembered. None of the other diners would recognise her. Santa Claus could walk in with Marilyn Monroe on his arm and no one would notice them. A waitress greeted her, and Charles waved and called out, "Over here, Agatha!"

"Shh!" she hissed as she bustled over to the table. "Don't make such a scene."

"What do you mean, sweetie? I wasn't making a scene."

"I don't want to attract attention," said Agatha, moving the candle on their table away from her. "I don't want anyone recognising me."

"Who do you think would recognise you?"

"I don't know — everyone. Apparently I'm known as 'the donkey lady.' "

"Ah, yes, I've heard about that."

"The entire planet has heard about it, Charles."

"You're not wrong there. Gustav showed me the social media internet stuff. You've gone viral."

"Oh, great. So now I'm not just a laughing stock, I'm a virus as well."

"It means that you're popular, Agatha. You

240

and your catchphrase."

"I have a catchphrase?"

"Yes. It used to be only you that said it. Now everyone is apparently saying 'snakes and bastards'!"

Agatha hid her face in her hands. "I can't stand it!" she said. "I thought I was going to be famous, not a figure of fun!"

"Hey, this isn't like you, sweetie. This is the kind of thing you normally wrestle into submission. I thought you would have shrugged it off by now."

"I had. I really had. I thought I had, anyway. But I don't want to be the donkey lady."

"On the bright side, not many people have such a good catchphrase."

"You're not funny, Charles — or is it really *Charlie* nowadays?"

"Mmm," Charles grunted, picking up the wine list. "You wouldn't like to change places with me, would you? I think I could cope with being the donkey lady better than I'm dealing with this whole marriage business. Let's order some wine."

They chose a bottle of Pinot Gris, and once the wine waiter was out of earshot, Agatha was first to speak.

"I'm not sure I'll ever be able to forgive you for not telling me about Mary straightaway," she said, "but I would like to know how you got yourself into this mess."

"It's not necessarily a *complete* mess," said Charles. "It's just a bit awkward. All to do with money, you see."

"But we got your finances on a fairly even keel," said Agatha. "The broker I put you in touch with — my own broker — is the best in the business. He had your investments ticking over nicely."

"Yes, but it was never really enough of an income," said Charles, "and then one of the chaps at my club put me on to what sounded like an unbeatable investment. A consortium mining for gold in the Amazon. Trouble is, they've now been told they can't do it. Too ecologically harmful, apparently. So until they find a way to extract the gold without destroying the rainforest and polluting the rivers, the gold is staying in the ground, and my money is buried with it.

"Then Mary's father contacted me. His little girl wants a certain lifestyle, and what Mary wants, she apparently gets."

"Amazing," said Agatha. "Aphrodite, Dinwiddy, and now Mary, all trying to use money to get men to give them what they want. The female of the species . . ."

"I don't follow you," said Charles, "but I am starting to think I've made a total hash of this. You were right when you said that the very people Mary wants to impress, the very set she aspires to join, are laughing at her behind her back. 'Bloody Mary' they're calling her, because of her family business in —"

"I get it."

"And 'the Brown-Field Sight' because she's not the most —"

"I get that, too."

"It's all rather irksome. I mean, I don't much care what they think or say — don't much care for them at all. But the Brown-Fields are going to force me to mix with them all the time. Gymkhanas and shooting weekends and riding with the hunt. Not that they're allowed to hunt anything nowadays. They just charge around the countryside on bloody great horses tooting horns and drinking port. It's not for me, Aggie. Not for me at all."

"And what does Gustav think of Mary?" Agatha already knew the answer. Gustav did not approve of Charles's relationship with Agatha. Gustav did not approve of Charles having a relationship with any woman who did not come from the right stock. To Gustav, breeding was everything, which was probably why he was so tight-lipped about his own mysterious foreign roots.

"Gustav despises Mary and her family, as I think you have probably already guessed. He is an utter snob. He thinks I should find a way out of this fiasco and call it all off."

"I agree with Gustav," said Agatha. "You should call it all off."

"Then that will be my mission," said Charles. "Let's drink to it."

They touched glasses and sipped the chilled white wine.

"So what about your murder case?"

Agatha brought Charles up to date on events at Morrison's as they ordered and ate their meal. He listened intently.

"And where does Chris Firkin fit into all this?" he asked eventually.

"He is like a breath of fresh air," said Agatha. "He is taking me to dinner on Friday night."

"I know," said Charles. "He told me. I felt like he was asking my permission."

"And you said . . . ?"

"I told him you were a free agent. You do as you please. No man can conquer Agatha Raisin."

"As if he would even want to try" — Agatha sighed — "to conquer the donkey lady."

"He would be mad *not* to try," said Charles, and there was an awkward pause when they both realised they were staring into each other's eyes. "Anyway, it could be worse," he said in a jolly voice, breaking the spell. "You could have been called 'the farting donkey lady.' "

"Too soon, Charles, too soon. I'm not ready to laugh about it yet."

They chatted for the rest of the evening like old friends, before, to save Charles the embarrassment of pretending that he had left his wallet in another jacket or on the side table in his bedroom, Agatha reneged on her promise to herself and insisted on paying. Outside the restaurant they hugged, and then, knowing she was losing the will to resist the urge to kiss him, she pushed him away and hurried to her car.

That night, as she rolled into bed, she felt very much alone, and she wished more than anything that Charles was with her. She strained to hear his car pulling up outside, or his footstep on the garden path, or the sound of his key, which she knew he still had, in the front door. She heard none of those things, and when she finally drifted off to sleep, she was still alone.

CHAPTER NINE

Agatha hurried down Carsely High Street, pulling her dark green woollen coat tight around her to ward off the morning chill. The heavy clouds that had rolled in over-night looked like they had sunk almost to the rooftops and were threatening the village with rain.

A bell tinkled merrily as she pushed open the door to the little café. Like so many others in Cotswold villages, this was an old-fashioned tea room with a scattering of tables covered with crisp white linen cloths. Carsely might have been bypassed to a large extent by the tourist trade, but the village tea room seemed to survive quite happily without the seasonal influx of touring coach parties and day trippers. On the counter at the back of the shop, Agatha fancied she could see a selection of muffins for toasting and an exotic display of croissants. Later in the day the shop would serve heavy fruit cake and light scones with afternoon tea. At this time of the morning, however, it was the smell of fresh coffee that filled the air.

She walked towards a vacant table. She knew that in this establishment there would be no choice of coffee with ridiculous names; no non-fat, one-pump, no-whip mocha, and certainly no ristretto, half-caff, dolce soy skinny latte with cinnamon. Here they served good coffee, black or white.

"Good morning, Mrs. Raisin," the woman behind the counter greeted her. "What would you like?" She was plump-faced, with a cheerful smile, and Agatha recognised her from her sporadic attendance at Carsely Ladies' Society meetings, though she could not remember her name.

"Morning," she replied. "Coffee, please. Best make that two. I have someone joining me."

A quick glance around the café had told her that Mary had not yet arrived. The handful of customers all looked towards her as she hung her coat on the back of her chair. The old couple near the window nodded and smiled. Two middle-aged women did likewise, and an elderly gentleman looked up from his paper and mouthed, "Good morning." Agatha listened hard for any whisper of "donkey lady" filtering through from the muted conversations in the room, but heard nothing. They might not be saying it, she thought, but they were certainly thinking it. Still, they seemed friendly enough. Her real adversary had yet to arrive.

The plump-faced woman placed two steaming cups of coffee on the table. "There's milk and cream in them little jugs," she said. "Just help yourself. Looks like we're going to have some rain, doesn't it?"

Agatha was saved from any exchange of pleasantries by the jolly tinkle of the bell. Mary Darlinda Brown-Field breezed in wearing a Burberry coat, carefully faded jeans, and fashionably fringed ankle boots.

"I am *so* sorry I'm late, Mrs. Raisin," she said, striding towards the table. Agatha checked the clock on the wall. It was only three minutes past ten.

"Don't be," she said. "You're not late at all."

"Oh, but I am," said Mary. "I always like to be punctual, but there is just so much to do at the moment. Simply *masses* to sort out for the wedding."

"I'm sure there is," said Agatha.

"Of course, I'm not really telling you anything, am I? You must know just what

I'm talking about. You've been through this whole thing a couple of times, haven't you?"

She might have quite a sweet smile, Agatha thought, if she didn't have a chin like an open sideboard drawer.

"Not, I'm sure, on the sort of scale that you are planning."

"Well, it really has to be quite a grand affair, I'm afraid," said Mary. "We have a great many business associates who are close personal friends, and of course, we have to invite all of Charlie's friends and they do expect these events to be of a certain standard, don't they?" She settled into her chair and sipped her coffee, then stirred in a little more cream.

"I very much doubt," said Agatha, "that Charles has his heart set on the sort of society wedding you are describing."

"Perhaps not," Mary said, her dark eyes meeting Agatha's, "but it's the bride's day. That's what they say, isn't it? It is my day and I will not let anything, or anyone, spoil it."

"Why would anyone want to do that?"

"Oh, there's always someone who might crop up and cause a problem." Mary lowered her voice to make sure that only Agatha could hear. "Of course, I won't have a drunken, blackmailing husband turn up to ruin the ceremony like you did. It really was most careless of you not to make sure that your first marriage was over before you launched into your second."

"You . . . you seem to know a lot about me."

"Know your enemy, Mrs. Raisin. That's another thing they say, isn't it? Know your enemy. I made it my business to find out all about you. You are not the only private detective for hire. My man turned up an awful lot of frightfully interesting stuff about your sordid little life."

Agatha felt a flush of anger. Had Charles actually been serious about marrying this woman?

Woman? She was really only a girl! She couldn't be more than twenty-two!

"He won't go through with it, you know," she said calmly, matching her younger opponent's soft tone. "Charles loathes that hunting, shooting, and fishing set. The horsey lot. They don't suit him at all . . . and neither do you."

"They may not suit him, Mrs. Raisin, but they suit me. I ride very well. It is my passion. I am also an excellent shot — deadly accurate with a shotgun or a rifle. Especially a rifle. I could put a round right in your eye from three hundred metres."

"Is that supposed to be a threat? Are you actually threatening me?"

"Take it however you like," hissed Mary, leaning close and speaking almost in a whisper. "I will have my way. Charles will do as he is told or I will ruin him. You will stay out of my way if you know what is good for you."

She doesn't want to make a scene, thought Agatha. She's trying to keep this nice and quiet. She doesn't want to be seen going head to head with me in public. She has a lot to learn.

"I don't take that sort of talk from a lantern-jawed, bug-eyed little shit like you," she whispered, then sprang to her feet. "What did you just call me?" she shrieked. "Bitch, was it? Why don't you slither off back to whatever slime pit you crawled out of, you disgusting little creature? Snakes and bastards! I've scraped better than you off my shoe! Now BUGGER OFF!"

Every face in the café turned towards them. Mary gave Agatha a look of sheer hatred, set her substantial jaw in a grimace and stormed out through the door. The little bell tinkled cheerfully.

Agatha looked round at the shocked customers. One of the middle-aged women was frozen with a cup halfway to her mouth.

A glob of marmalade from his slice of toast plopped into the elderly gentleman's newspaper.

"The donkey lady strikes again!" Agatha proclaimed, then sat down to finish her coffee.

Agatha was walking along Lilac Lane to where she had parked her car when the gloom of the morning was suddenly illuminated by a flash of lightning that split the sky. An instant later, she felt the breath squeezed from her chest when the loudest boom of thunder she had ever heard shook the air. She quickened her pace, diving into her car as the first huge splots of rain hit the windscreen.

Driving up the hill to take the road towards Mircester, the rain began to fall much harder, and by the time she was out on the main road, it was coming down in torrents. The windscreen wipers were struggling to cope, and what she could see up ahead looked more like a river than a road. Deciding that she would rather sit out the cloudburst than land upside down in a ditch, she pulled into the car park of a pub called the Greedy Goose. More than once, she and Charles had enjoyed a long, lazy Sunday lunch there before heading back to Carsely for a long, energetic Sunday evening in Lilac Lane. The rain drummed on the roof of the car and bounced off the bonnet. What was he thinking of, marrying that dreadful girl? Money, of course, but there was more to life than money . . . and what did Mary mean when she said that she would ruin him? Did the Brown-Fields really have that much of a financial stranglehold on him already? He simply had to get out of the marriage. That girl was a truly nasty piece of work.

Agatha turned her mind to the Morrison affair. Money was at the root of that sordid business as well, and it had turned into a personal vendetta. Because of Albert Morrison, Agatha had been humiliated on national television. She had a score to settle with him over that, but more important was the murder of Clarissa Dinwiddy. Trotter had done it, but the others were in on it, Agatha was sure of that. If only for the sake of poor Elizabeth Thirkettle, she was determined to prove that Morrison and his chums had murdered Mrs. Dinwiddy.

The rain had begun to ease off. Agatha started the car and pulled out onto the main road, heading for the office.

"Come on, Toni, what have you got for

me?" called Agatha, striding across the outer office. "You must have turned up something else by now."

"Not much," said Toni, sounding glum. "A couple of more interesting snippets, but it's all mainly domestic drudgery."

"Well, leave your drudgery out here and bring your interesting bits into my office," said Agatha. "We'll have a listen to it all in there. I'll fire up my computer. No, don't tell me . . . I can remember how to do it."

By the time Toni appeared in the office doorway with a computer memory stick in her hand, Agatha had almost managed to switch on her machine. She allowed Toni to hustle her out of the way and finish the job.

"I'm down to the last few folders now," said Toni. "I think I'll have finished listening to it all by this evening. These are the only new ones that are of any interest."

"I don't want anything going wrong with the big shipment."

"That's Morrison."

"I will check the buildings along with Bream and Dunster to make sure everything is secure."

"And that is Sayer."

"Fine, but once we take delivery we will need everyone to lend a hand."

"Morrison again," said Agatha. "This is

254

good stuff, Toni."

"No problem. I will get them to confirm the ETA. Could be as soon as next Thursday."

"Sayer again . . ." Agatha paused. "ETA — that's estimated time of arrival. When was this recorded, Toni?"

"It's difficult to tell," Toni explained. "Mrs. Dinwiddy was really organised about the way she stored these files, but what appear to be the later ones are a bit jumbled up, almost like she was trying to disguise them, or hide them amongst the rest of the mundane stuff. She hasn't been consistent, though. Maybe she wasn't thinking straight. It's all a bit of a mess."

"You said 'later ones.' How recent are they?"

"I think most of them are probably within the last couple of weeks."

"Really? Toni, this is dynamite!" Agatha gasped. "If this was recorded within the last couple of weeks and Sayer was talking about Thursday — today is Thursday. Their big shipment could be tonight!"

"Yes, I suppose that is possible . . ."

"You suppose?" said Agatha. "Toni, I don't think Clarissa Dinwiddy is the only one who wasn't thinking straight on this. What's wrong with you? Get it together, girl. What are you dreaming about? You need to keep your mind on the job and . . . This is about that bloke you're seeing, isn't it?"

"Seeing him? When do you think I've had time to see anybody, let alone him? I've been stuck listening to hours and hours of this prattling gossip for days and days!"

"That's your job!"

"How is listening to a load of depressing old crap my job?"

"Because you are a detective and this is a murder!"

"My job is NOT to be a murder detective!"

"Your job is what I say it is!"

"Well maybe you should just shove your job up your —"

"You've split up with him, haven't you?"

"We did NOT split up!" Toni, having swelled with indignation, slowly deflated again. "I told him that I wasn't ready to get married . . . that there were other things I still wanted to do."

"Oh . . ." said Agatha, barely able to conceal a fist-pumping whoop. Toni is staying with me! She isn't going to run off, start breeding, and become overwhelmed by the horrendous tidal wave of a squeaky-clean young family! "You poor thing. That's a tough call to make. It must have been . . .

um . . . really hard on him?"

"That's what I thought." Toni shook her head and then surprised Agatha by managing a smile. "But he said that working for a detective agency was miles more interesting than anything he could offer. He said that if that's what makes me happy, then it's what I should do, because if I'm not happy then our marriage would be doomed."

"Who is this guy?" said Agatha. "Your average man doesn't think like that. Are you sure you want to let him go?"

"I'm not letting him go," Toni explained. "I'm just keeping him where I need him to be — where he and I both need to be. Some way down the line, things may change."

That, thought Agatha, is the best news I have heard all day. Now that she's got it all off her chest, maybe she'll start sparking like I need her to. I can't afford to let her go all mushy on me. I need her operating at full capacity.

"And then," said Toni, "we had a bit of a laugh when he said, 'After all, how could I compete with the donkey lady?' That's quite funny, isn't it?"

"Of course," said Agatha, forcing a smile. "The whole donkey lady thing is . . . really very funny."

"And then he said . . ." — Toni held her

hand to her mouth to stifle a giggle — "that you had your own catchphrase where you said —"

"Don't push it," Agatha interrupted. "Get back to the last of those recordings."

That night Agatha drove to the pineapple gates of Albert Morrison's manor house and pulled her car into a parking spot on the main road close by. She had decided that it would be easier to take a look at the factory from this direction rather than approaching from the main factory gates. She promised herself that she would not do anything silly. All I need to do, she told herself, is check if there are any lights on in the factory — check if there's anything going on that could mean that tonight is the night for Morrison's "big shipment."

She crept in through the gates and made her way up the drive towards the stables, flitting between the moon shadows cast by the trees. She was wearing walking shoes, black trousers, and a heavy black sweater to blend into the darkness. She knew she would be difficult to spot, but she was keeping a wary eye for any potential sentries prowling the grounds.

Skirting past the stable block, she quickly reached the R&D building. She flattened herself against the wall and slowly poked her head around the corner to look across to the main building. Sure enough, there were lights on. The windows were covered with blinds, but they did not mask the glow from inside.

I know I'm not going to do anything silly, she reminded herself, but I *have* to see what's going on in there. It's not as if they'll be expecting visitors. They will have searched the whole place and locked all the doors so that they can concentrate on whatever it is they are up to. The doors might all be locked, but . . . She patted the pocket containing the key that Toni had given her. All she needed to do was to take a very quick look. She'd be in and out of there without them ever knowing a thing.

Getting into the R&D building was, as Toni had described, perfectly simple. Most of the doors and windows were missing. Agatha fished a slim penlight out of her pocket. The majority of the building was blackened and burned, and the floor was littered with debris. Her flashlight cast eerie shadows across the floor as she picked her way towards the door to the ladies' lavatory. Just as Toni had said, it looked like it was locked. She gave it a gentle push. Nothing happened. She shoved harder and, with a slight crunching sound, the door opened. She played her torch beam over the charred frame and could see where part of it had broken away, clinging shakily to the lock and the edge of the door. Being careful not to do any further damage, she slipped inside and eased the door closed behind her.

Inside, the lavatory seemed largely unaffected by the fire. Scanning the room with her penlight, she quickly found the door that linked to the ladies' lavatory in the main building. She tried the key in the lock. It turned with a soft click. She inched the door open, expecting at any moment to have it torn out of her hands by Bream or Dunster on the other side. She breathed a small sigh of relief when she could see that the room beyond the door was in darkness. Of course it was, she told herself. Why would any of those blokes be using the ladies' loo? She locked the door behind her and crossed the floor to where another door would take her into the main building, opening it just a crack. Outside was a corridor, fully lit. She chanced a glance left and then right. The coast was clear. A few yards down the corridor was the door to the dispatch department.

This, Agatha warned herself, was the really tricky bit. She tried the handle and gently opened the door just far enough to see inside. Five figures clad in white stood at a long workbench. They were wearing the same sort of forensic overalls that Bill Wong had donned when he went to fish the false leg out of the undergrowth. They were also wearing white latex gloves and white nuisance masks over their faces. Bream, Dunster, Sayer, Trotter, and Morrison, thought Agatha. I would recognise them anywhere, despite what they're wearing.

The five of them were unpacking boxes filled with batteries about the size of a large soup can. They were then using tools like small bolt cutters to slice open the batteries and remove plastic-wrapped packages from the inside. Those packages were then being cut open and the powdery substance inside poured into larger plastic bags, making bigger packages.

We were right, Agatha congratulated herself. They are shipping drugs into the country in those batteries! She felt a strange vibration tingling her right buttock. What's that? she wondered. Not entirely unpleasant, but . . . SNAKES AND BASTARDS! My phone! She scrabbled to retrieve it from her back pocket just as the first shrill ring filled the air. She stabbed at the screen to answer the call and cut off the sound.

"Not now, Toni!" she hissed, quickly ending the call, but she had not been quick enough.

"What was that?" Morrison looked up from the workbench. "There's someone in here! Get them!"

Bream and Dunster were already heading towards her. Agatha dashed back to the ladies' lavatory, closing the door behind her. It was dark. She fumbled for the key to unlock her escape route, but it slipped through her fingers and she heard the metallic clink as it hit the floor and bounced. Risking a quick flash of her penlight, she immediately spotted it under the door into one of the cubicles. She dodged inside to retrieve it at the very moment that the lights were suddenly turned on.

"Who's in here?"

It was Dunster. A chill of dread shot down Agatha's spine. She stood absolutely still, not even daring to breathe. There was the crash of a cubicle door being flung open, followed by another, followed by another, followed by . . . hers.

"Caught short, were we, Mrs. Raisin?"

Dunster reached in and grabbed her by the hair, dragging her out of the cubicle. She screamed, punched, slapped, and clawed at his face, but he flung her to the floor.

"Well, well, what have we here?" Bream had entered the room. He lifted Agatha to her feet and twisted her right arm behind her back.

"That hurts, you bastard!"

"It's meant to — now move!"

Bream marched Agatha back along the corridor to the dispatch department with Dunster following on behind. Albert Morrison was pacing the floor when they entered. He had removed his mask, and Agatha watched his lips tighten into an ugly snarl when he saw her.

"You!" he roared. "I might have known. Well, this is the last time you'll be sticking your nose into my business, you infuriating woman. I can guarantee that!"

"And what a sordid business it is," said Agatha. "Drugs? Murder? You were supposed to be on the verge of a major breakthrough with that new battery pack. You might actually have achieved something remarkable. Instead, you have become nothing better than a gangster with a bunch of hired thugs working for you."

Bream shoved her forward, letting go of her arm. Free of his grasp, she spun round, ready to make a break for the door, but

Dunster stood in her way, an ugly little automatic pistol in his hand, pointed straight at her. She looked at his face. A livid red weal had erupted from his cheekbone to his chin where she had gouged him with her nails. He touched it tenderly with the fingertips of his free hand.

"A bit sore, is it?" Agatha asked. "Give me a chance and I'll do you one to match on the other side."

"That's really not going to happen," he said, aiming the pistol at her head. "You're dead meat."

"Not here," barked Morrison, "and not now. We have work to do."

"Arms out," ordered Sayer, grabbing Agatha's wrist and yanking one arm out level with her shoulder. He ran his hands over her arms and down her back, searching her. He lingered a little on her breasts, giving her a nod of approval.

"Teach you that in officer training, did they, Lieutenant Webster?" Agatha goaded him.

He frowned at her.

"Oh, we know all about you," she continued. "The police do too. They'll be here any second," she lied, trying to think of anything that would save her skin. "That was what the phone call was about. You don't stand a chance."

Sayer had found the phone in her back pocket and was flicking the buttons.

"One-two-three-four-five? Not a very secure password." He smiled, then turned to Morrison. "That was an incoming call from her sidekick. Lasted less than two seconds. She didn't have time to tell her anything. There's no one coming."

Morrison picked up a roll of packing tape and threw it to Trotter. "Make sure she can't move," he said, "and start with her mouth. I don't want to hear another word out of her. Bream, Dunster, search the whole area. Check that she didn't bring any of her friends with her. Then get back in here. Once we're finished with the shipment, you can do what you like with her. Trotter, use that old Land Rover and take her out into the woods somewhere. Somewhere miles from here. Make sure the body is never found."

"She must have come here by car," said Sayer. "Find it. We'll have to dispose of that, too."

"You won't get away with this, Morrison!" Agatha yelled. "You're nothing but a —" And then Trotter clamped a strip of packing tape over her mouth, winding the roll around her head to silence her. Bream held her arms while Trotter bound her wrists. They shoved her onto the floor in the corner of the room and Trotter stooped to bind her ankles. She aimed a kick at his head, but he dodged back and Bream slapped her hard across the face.

"Just behave," he warned, "or this will get really nasty."

Trussed and gagged, barely able to breathe, Agatha slumped in the corner. Hot tears of anger and fear welled in her eyes. Was this it? Was this how she was to spend the last moments of her life? Why, oh why had she thought she could spy on these monsters and get away with it? But most of all, she thought, over and over, she did not want to die.

Morrison and Trotter replaced their masks and went back to work. Sayer issued Bream and Dunster with a few more instructions, then he also returned to the workbench. The two security guards were gone for almost an hour. Agatha watched as the pile of fresh packages at the end of the bench continued to grow. Every battery that was sliced open, every bag that was added to the pile marked one more pendulum swing on the clock counting down to the end of her life.

Eventually Bream and Dunster returned, and Trotter brought in a collection of large black holdalls and began filling them with the packages. The mangled battery carcasses were swept into sacks for disposal. Morrison removed his mask and motioned Trotter to stop.

"Leave that," he said. "Sayer and I will sort it out. You three deal with her."

"I'll get her car," said Bream, struggling out of his white overalls and stuffing them into one of the sacks. "I'll follow on behind you."

"What we gonna do with the tart?" said Trotter.

"We'll have to carry her," said Dunster.

"Well *I* ain't carryin' her," Trotter snorted, bending down and cutting the tape around Agatha's ankles. "She can bloody well walk, and if she tries anythin', she'll get some of this!" He prodded his fist into her forehead, hard enough to hurt but not hard enough to knock her senseless.

Dunster and Trotter forced her out into the night. She could feel Dunster's steely grip around her upper arm, alternately shoving and hauling her towards the stable yard. Trotter held a powerful flashlight that lit their way and, when they reached the stables, illuminated the battered old Land Rover.

"We're gonna have some fun in the back

267

there." He grinned. "How about that, eh? Mrs. Agatha Raisin, the great detective, and little Peter Trotter havin' a grand old time in the back of my Land Rover! How does that grab you?"

Agatha's eyes narrowed and she howled at him through the packing tape gag.

"What was that?" Trotter laughed. "I couldn't quite hear you there." He ripped the tape roughly from her face.

"NEVER!" she screamed. "NEVER!!"

Suddenly there came a low growl, rumbling out of the darkness. Trotter spun round and his flashlight beam picked up two glowing red eyes. There was a deafening "Hee-haw!" and Wizz-Wazz charged. She butted the surprised Dunster in the chest, sending him sprawling across the yard, and flicked a vicious kick into Trotter's stomach that left him doubled over in agony. Agatha bolted into the darkness. She crashed into the door of Wizz-Wazz's loose box and stumbled through, her hands still taped firmly behind her back.

"Where the hell did she go?" yelled Dunster.

Agatha cowered in the darkness.

"Get me that flashlight!" he ordered.

"I . . . can't move," groaned Trotter. There was another raucous "Hee-haw!" and a squeal of pain.

From her hiding place, Agatha could see the flashlight beam sweeping the stable yard.

"Come out now, you stupid bitch," Dunster shouted, "or it will be worse for you in the end."

There was a clattering of hooves on the cobbles, a thumping sound, and a groan from Dunster.

"Damn that animal," he cursed, and a shot rang out.

Agatha watched as the beam illuminated one area of the yard after another. Dunster was searching for her. Still unable to loosen her hands, she squirmed and wriggled in the straw at the back of the loose box, burrowing her way in. Finally convinced that she was completely covered, she peered out from under the straw, trembling, terrified. The flashlight lit up the loose box next to hers, then turned towards her.

"I know you're in there," Dunster shouted. "Don't make me come in after you."

Agatha closed her eyes and stayed as still as her shivers of fear would allow.

"Right," spat Dunster, taking a step forward. "Now you're for it."

Suddenly the entire stable yard was flooded with bright white light, and a deep voice boomed over a loudspeaker: "Armed police! Put down your weapon! Armed police! On the ground, NOW!"

Dunster put his hands in the air. He dropped his pistol, backed out of the loose box and sank to his knees.

"Armed police! Stay where you are! Do NOT move!"

Two police officers carrying pistols swooped on Dunster. One of them kept him covered while the other retrieved his gun. Then the familiar figure of Bill Wong appeared, silhouetted in the bright light. He grabbed one of Dunster's wrists and then the other, snapping handcuffs into place, then turned to the loose box.

"Are you in there, Agatha?" he called. "Are you okay?"

Agatha Raisin emerged from her hiding place, staggering towards the light, her hair, face, and clothes covered in damp straw and donkey shit.

"Oh, thank goodness!" Toni appeared from behind Bill Wong and threw her arms around her boss. Bill cut the tape on Agatha's wrists.

"I'm okay," Agatha whispered. "I'm alive . . ."

Then she felt the familiar coarse, spiky touch of donkey hair as Wizz-Wazz tucked

her head under her arm and gave a soft
whicker of affection.

CHAPTER TEN

"I really just want to go home and get cleaned up," Agatha complained. She was sitting in the back of an ambulance, a red blanket draped over her shoulders. The paramedics had given her a thorough check and confirmed to Bill Wong that she was physically unharmed.

"Of course you do," said Bill, with heartfelt sympathy, "and I will drive you home myself. We need you to stay here for a while longer, though, until we have cleared everything up."

"I can stay with you tonight, if you like," said Toni. "You shouldn't be on your own after all this."

"Or we can have an officer stay at your house," said Bill. "I'm sure Alice would be only too happy to oblige."

"No, we needn't trouble Alice," said Agatha. "Toni, if you would stay with me, that would be very kind."

A uniformed officer appeared and spoke quietly to Bill, who nodded, then turned to Agatha.

"Okay," he said. "The site is secure and our boys can carry on gathering evidence, but there's no need for us to keep you here. Bream was collared trying to use your car to get away. He rammed a police vehicle. Your car is a bit of a mess."

"I don't much care about the car," said Agatha. "As long as you got *him.*"

"He's safely under lock and key," Bill confirmed. "I can fill you in on the rest back at your place. Come on." He offered Agatha his hand to support her as she stepped down from the back of the ambulance.

"Just a minute!" came the instantly recognisable bark of Chief Inspector Wilkes. "I want a word with you! I have warned you time and time again about interfering in police matters. Well, this time your meddling almost had dire consequences, didn't it? This time, your amateur bungling nearly got you killed! If it were up to me —"

"Oh, shut your face, you stupid man!" Agatha looked on in surprise as Toni rounded on the chief inspector. "Fortunately, it's not up to you, so why don't you shove off back to whatever hole you crawl into at night? You wouldn't know a criminal if you caught one pinching the boots off your feet. Agatha is responsible for catching an entire gang of them here tonight!"

"She's right, sir," said Bill. "Mrs. Raisin has exposed a major drug-smuggling operation and solved a murder that we were fooled into thinking was an accident. She deserves a great deal of credit for sticking to her guns and seeing this whole thing through."

"You'd best be careful, Sergeant," Wilkes said, waving a finger at him. "You're treading on thin ice."

"Don't take this out on him." Toni leapt to Bill's defence. "You're the one who was willing to let these thugs get away with murder!"

"You can't speak to me like that, you little —"

"I'll talk to you any way I like, you miserable old pillock!"

Wilkes grunted with fury, his eyes darting from Toni to Agatha, who returned his stare impassively. Then he turned and marched off, muttering to himself.

"Not bad," said Agatha, nodding to Toni, "for an apprentice donkey lady."

Agatha could hear the crackle of the police radio from the car parked outside her cottage. She walked downstairs, having show-ered, slipped into a long bathrobe and reap-plied enough make-up to make herself look presentable. Even at this late hour, she knew that the presence of the police vehicle in Lilac Lane, parked just behind Toni's little car, would be attracting attention. Carsely's spy network would be on red alert. Before morning, the story of how Agatha Raisin was brought home in a police car would be all round the village. Yes, the curtains would certainly be twitching out there tonight. Not those at James Lacey's windows, of course. There was still no sign of him. He was abroad somewhere, mixing travel writing with military history, probably on an ancient battlefield that no one had ever heard of. Apart from those who died there, of course — but they weren't telling. She had tried ringing Charles, but there was no sign of him, either. Doubtless his ghastly fiancée had him on a tight leash. She would have him cornered in one of the many rooms in Barfield House, bombarding him with guest lists, seating plans, menu options, and colour swatches. Or maybe not. Maybe Charles had found somewhere to hide from her. Maybe he had burrowed into the straw as well.

The moment Agatha walked into the living room, Toni slotted a glass of brandy into her hand. Then she poured one for herself and they sat together on the sofa. Bill Wong settled into an armchair with a mug of tea.

"You have no idea how grateful I am to both of you," Agatha said. "That was the most terrifying thing that's ever happened to me."

"I'm sure it was," said Toni gently. "But it's over now."

"How did you know where I was? I didn't tell anyone I was going to the factory. I wouldn't have gone in there at all if I hadn't seen the lights on."

"I heard Morrison's voice before you rang off," Toni explained. "I was still in the office, working my way through the last of the recordings, and I noticed that the key I stole wasn't where you'd left it on your desk. Tonight of all nights, Morrison's was the only place you could be."

"But how did you manage to call in half the cops in the county?"

"It was pretty clear from what Toni let me hear that we needed a full team on this — including armed officers," said Bill.

"Wow," said Agatha. "Just what did you find on those final recordings?"

"Everything that we'd been looking for," said Toni, placing on the coffee table in front of them a small digital recorder similar to the one used by Clarissa Dinwiddy. "I copied the relevant files onto here. This is Morrison."

"*I heard on the news that the Americans have bombed another ten processing plants in Helmand. They're going to blow this business to pieces!*"

"And now Sayer," she added.

"*That will have practically no effect on production at all. The Afghans can set up a new lab within days. They already have hundreds of them. The heroin will keep on coming — as much of it as we can handle.*"

"These recordings came later. First Sayer."

"*The big shipment is en route. It will be here on Thursday night.*"

"Then Bream."

"*Shouldn't we be cooling things down a bit? I mean, this Raisin woman is attracting far more attention over the fake leg than we thought. We should back off a bit.*"

"*Back off? Would you like to tell that to our friends in Afghanistan? Or Sekiliv? What do you think they would do if we told them we had to shut everything down because of some crazy woman?*"

"That was Sayer."

"*They don't know how things work here . . .*"

"Bream, and then Sayer again."

"And they don't care! Any hint of us getting cold feet and one of their enforcers will show up here quicker than you can say Kalashnikov. He will get rid of Raisin and we'll be next on his list. There is too much money at stake for us to let anything go wrong. If needs be, we will have to take care of Raisin ourselves. Make sure you, Dunster and Trotter are here on Thursday. Morrison will be here too. It will take all of us to clear the goods before morning."

"That explains why Clarissa Dinwiddy was so frightened of Morrison's thugs," said Agatha. "She must have taken some serious risks to record that stuff."

"A risk too far in the end," Bill confirmed. "We're getting it all from Peter Trotter. He's in hospital. Badly broken ribs. That donkey really didn't like him, did she?"

"There's nothing to like," said Agatha. "He is a loathsome little man."

"He's been talking to Alice, who is sitting by his hospital bed taking notes. Trotter is determined that he's not going to take all the blame for the murder. He's telling us everything in the hope that he'll get a lighter sentence. He has confessed to killing Clarissa Dinwiddy with the ashtray."

"Because she knew too much?" asked Agatha.

"Exactly," said Bill. "On the day of her murder, she confronted Albert Morrison and played him the conversations she had on her recorder. She told him that she knew he wasn't a bad man at heart and begged him to leave Aphrodite, abandon the drugs business and run off with her somewhere safe, where they could settle down together.

"But she was wrong. He is a very bad man. He came up with the plan to kill her. He knew that she visited the donkey regularly to check she was being properly looked after. He also knew that Trotter hated Mrs. Dinwiddy enough to kill her."

"So they got Trotter to do their dirty work for them," said Agatha, "while they all had perfect alibis, seen by everyone at Aphrodite's homecoming party."

"I think they saw Trotter as being expendable," said Toni. "If anything went wrong, he would be the one facing a murder charge. He wasn't originally part of their gang. He was hired to look after Wizz-Wazz, but it soon became clear that they could use him as a general dogsbody, and he was keen enough when he realised how much money was involved."

"At the party," Agatha recalled, "Morrison

looked right at me when he ordered Sayer to tell Clarissa to go to the stables. I think . . . I think he was *hoping* I would go down there. Hoping that I would be the one to find the body."

"Probably," said Bill. "We know that you were hired, as you guessed, for show. After his dodgy battery pack caused the fire, Morrison wanted to make it look like industrial espionage. To make it appear that he believed that, he needed to be seen to do something about it, so he hired you. The fake leg stunt was to discredit you and give him the chance to sack you. If you could also discover the 'accident' set up by Trotter, I think he hoped you might somehow take some of the blame for that, too. It would make sacking you even easier."

"Well, I'm glad Trotter is suffering," said Agatha. "He deserves everything Wizz-Wazz gave him, and more. What about Dunster?"

"Not badly hurt," Bill said. "A few bruises. He's made of sterner stuff than Trotter."

"And Wizz-Wazz? She seemed fine when she came over to me," Agatha said, "but I heard a shot."

"That was just Dunster firing wildly into the darkness," Toni said. "He was trying to frighten her off, but he didn't hit her."

"What about Morrison?" asked Agatha.

"Our men caught him leaving the factory with the heroin," said Bill. "He is going to prison for a very long time. Sadly, there was no sign of Sayer. We're still looking, but he has slipped through our fingers for the time being."

"The survival expert," Agatha snorted, "survives yet again."

"He was key to the whole operation," said Bill. "When Bream went missing in Afghanistan, he made a few initial contacts with the drugs barons, but Sayer faked his own death so that he could work with those people. He travelled the whole route from Helmand to Eastern Europe and back to the UK, setting up all the connections they would need along the way, doing all the deals that would take them across borders and through territories controlled by some extremely dangerous characters."

"None of those people are going to be very happy that it's all gone wrong," said Toni.

"They will always find some other way of plying their filthy trade," Agatha said. "This little network may have closed down, but they will find others."

"That, I'm afraid, is almost inevitable," Bill agreed. "Now, I must leave you ladies in peace. I need to get back to the station.

There is a mountain of paperwork to get through. Which reminds me, Agatha, I will send a car for you in the morning so that you can make a formal statement down at the station."

After Bill had left, Toni and Agatha sat together on the sofa finishing their drinks.

"We've had our ups and downs recently," Agatha said, "but I honestly don't know anyone I can rely on more than you to back me up, to be there for me when the going gets tough."

"I'm glad you think that," said Toni, "because when I thought they might have . . ." A tear forced its way out of her eye and rolled down her cheek.

"Oh, don't start that" — Agatha sighed — "or you'll get me going, too."

"Sorry," said Toni. "We're detectives. We have to be tough. We have to look out for one another. That's what friends are for."

"Come on, I'm exhausted. Time for bed. You're in the spare room. In the morning, I'll lend you clean knickers," said Agatha, dragging herself to her feet. "And you're right — that is what friends are for."

"What — clean knickers?"

"That, too."

Bright and early next morning, having

shared a pot of coffee with Agatha, Toni set off for work. No more sound files to wade through, but she had to catch up on what was happening with the agency's other cases. She would need to keep on top of things while Agatha was out of the office. After all, she was working for the most famous private detective in the country. She was proud to be young, single, and an independent woman. She was proud to be a private investigator, and she was proud to be wearing Agatha Raisin's knickers. I may not be able to fill her shoes yet, she thought, or even her underwear for that matter, but one day, one day . . .

Agatha watched Toni strutting down the path, looking full of confidence and vigour. She still felt tired from the night before and knew that she had hours of tedious questions ahead of her once the car arrived to take her to Mircester police station. She cast her eye around the room, wondering what to do until the car showed up. There was an ashtray sitting on a side table. An ashtray. An ashtray had killed Clarissa Dinwiddy, and had nearly killed Agatha, too. In the not-too-distant past, she would have sat down and enjoyed a cigarette while waiting for the car. Now, she never wanted to see another ashtray again. She hated the things.

She tucked the offending item into a drawer, out of sight. A hatred of ashtrays, she decided, was just the thing to ensure that she never smoked again.

It was after lunchtime when Agatha was once again standing at the window of her living room, looking out at the gloomy sky of a grey autumn day. She had, as expected, spent hours at the police station and had asked to be brought home afterwards so that she could rest and decide what to wear to dinner. Tonight, after all, Chris Firkin was taking her out, and she wanted to look her best. Just then, a pink sports car drew up outside her house. A blonde woman emerged from the car. She was wearing a pink fun-fur coat not unlike the one that Agatha had donated to Wizz-Wazz, although the colour of Agatha's coat had not matched the paintwork of her car. Aphrodite Morrison strolled towards the front door, removing her dark sunglasses — presumably because it was so dull out there that she couldn't see a thing. Agatha hurried out to open the door.

"Mrs. Morrison, I wasn't expecting you."

"Yous kin make dat Aphrodite, Mrs. . . . can I just say Agatha?"

"Of course," said Agatha. "Do, please,

come in."

Aphrodite took three steps across the hall into the living room.

"Cute," she said, looking round the room.

"Can I get you something?" Agatha asked. "A drink . . . er . . . tea maybe?"

"Naw, I'm good," Aphrodite sat on the sofa, where Agatha joined her. "I wanna talk to yous about dat no-good husband of mine."

"He's not exactly my favourite person."

"My neither. I got my lawyers on him. I'm gonna sue his ass to hell and back. By the time he gets out of jail, he's gonna have nothin'. I'm takin' the house, the factory, the stables, everythin'."

"What will you do with Wizz-Wazz?"

"I've always had a soft spot for dat mad donkey. Never saw too much of her before, but now she's gonna be a star. There's a company plannin' a toy range and I'm gonna get them to set up in the factory. That way we can keep the employees that wanna stay. The stables and the grounds are gonna be turned into the Clarissa Dinwiddy Donkey Sanctuary, so I'm gonna get a whole bunch more donkeys dat need some TLC."

"It's very generous of you to name the sanctuary after Mrs. Dinwiddy. I didn't think you were friends."

"We weren't. We never got on. She wanted my husband, you know. Wanted him to leave me. She paid off that tart on reception. She even made sure that they never hired any other good-lookin' young girls that might take his eye. She only let them hire ugly mugs."

"Like the trapeze girl?"

"The what?"

"It doesn't matter."

"Anyways, even if we wasn't the best of friends, there ain't no way that Dinwiddy deserved what he done to her. So I'm gonna set up the factory and the sanctuary, and if I keep my mind on that, maybe it will help keep me off the sauce. So I got you to thank for that — here."

Aphrodite reached inside her jacket and produced a white envelope, holding it out to Agatha.

"What is it?" Agatha asked, reaching for it.

"It's a cheque," said Aphrodite. "Kinda old-fashioned nowadays, writin' cheques, but dat's what it is. Should cover your fee plus a little more for expenses and all the trouble you went to."

"You don't have to . . ."

"Take it. Yous got people to pay and I can afford it, so just take it." She stood and

286

made for the door. "An' any time yous want to come visit, just you rock on up to the stables," she added. "Wizz-Wazz would love that. After all, you's the donkey lady, ain't ya?"

"Yes." Agatha smiled. "I suppose I am."

She watched Aphrodite glide back down the path towards her pink car. Without the voice, she thought, she was the essence of glamour, although the coat and the car . . . Well, they weren't to Agatha's taste, but they certainly made an impact.

"How very sweet," came a voice.

She spun round to see John Sayer standing in her living room.

"How did you . . . ?"

"I walked in through your open back door, Mrs. Raisin, while you were busy with the lovely Aphrodite."

"What are you doing here?"

"I came to see you. You threw a mighty big spanner in the works and brought our whole operation crashing down. You have cost me an awful lot of money. I wanted you to know that. I wanted you to know how much I hate you for it . . . before I kill you."

"You must be mad coming here! Don't you know that —"

Sayer clamped his right hand around Agatha's throat and hurled her backwards into the armchair.

"Have a seat, Mrs. Raisin, and tell me what I don't know."

Agatha massaged her aching neck and said hoarsely, "Don't you know that every policeman in the country is looking for you. Not to mention the military police, and probably your friends from Afghanistan and Eastern Europe, too."

"None of them will ever find me. I'm a survival expert, Mrs. Raisin. Out in the wild or in the busiest of towns, I know how to merge in and disappear. Escape and evasion is what we called it in the army."

"You've come a long way since your days in uniform," Agatha said. "But why here? How did Morrison get involved?"

"He had established a small factory in Sekiliv. It was one of a number of legitimate firms I was looking at. Initially we wanted to find a way to infiltrate the business and set up our own operation without anyone else knowing. I met Morrison in Sekiliv when he was there on business and I was posing as a buyer for a company in Spain. It didn't take me long to persuade him that there was more money to be made in our business than in his, especially once I found out that his firm was on the verge of col-

288

lapse. His useless battery pack had pretty much bankrupted him."

"And now he's in jail, which is a better option than living life on the run. How long can you go on looking over your shoulder, wondering whether it will be a policeman or a hit man who finally catches up with you?"

"That's not your problem, Mrs. Raisin. All *your* problems are now over."

Sayer advanced towards Agatha. She squirmed sideways to try to dodge him as he reached down to grab her.

"Leave her alone!" She looked up to see that Chris Firkin had walked into the room.

"Who the hell are you?" said Sayer.

"What do you care?" said Chris. "Just leave her alone and try picking on someone your own size."

"I will," Sayer promised, stepping towards him.

"I'm not scared of you," Chris said defiantly.

"You should be," said Sayer.

Agatha watched Sayer cover the distance between himself and Chris in the blink of an eye. His speed of movement was matched by the speed with which he rained blows on his opponent. Chris blocked one punch and ducked away from another but took a ferocious thump to the eye followed by another to the mouth. Sayer skipped back lightly and flicked a kick into Chris's ribs that sent him staggering back past the open living room door to crash into the wall by the window. His knees buckled and he sank towards the floor before recovering and starting to pull himself upright.

"Is that the best you've got?" He spat blood from his cut lip.

"Far from it."

As Sayer moved swiftly towards Chris, Agatha charged across the room wielding a side table, which she smashed into his back. The table splintered, but Sayer was still standing, seemingly unaffected. He half turned, holding up a clenched fist.

"You shouldn't have —" he started to say, just as a large orange frying pan appeared from beyond the door, smacking him square in the face. Agatha recognised the pan straight away. It was Le Creuset, part of a set she had bought to hang on hooks in the kitchen, more as ornaments than anything else given her lamentable cooking skills. The blow left Sayer dazed, and a second, sharp smack with the pan sent him to the floor. Then Sir Charles Fraith dived on top of him.

"Get his feet, Chris!" he yelled.

Chris obediently fell forward onto Sayer's legs. Then Charlotte Clark darted in, armed with a roll of cling film. That, too, Agatha recognised from her kitchen. She used it to cover things in dishes before she blasted them in the microwave. The groggy Sayer, blood streaming from his nose, made little objection as they wrapped his ankles in cling film and then did the same to his torso, pinning his arms to his sides.

"Where did you three spring from?" asked Agatha.

"I came to talk about my exclusive, Mrs. Raisin," said Charlotte, "but I was walking up the path when I saw this guy with his hand around your throat, so I ran off to get help."

"And she found us," said Charles, handing Chris a handkerchief to staunch the flow of blood from his eyebrow. "Chris had taken me for a spin in his zingy little electric car. We were heading to the Red Lion to discuss an extension to his lease when this young lady flagged us down."

"Why didn't you just call the police straightaway?" Agatha asked Charlotte.

"It's my phone," said Charlotte. "No power — a dodgy battery."

"Unlike my car," Chris said, pressing the handkerchief to his eyebrow. "Which brought us silently to your garden gate. I volunteered to keep Sayer occupied while Charles lay in ambush behind the door."

The arrival of the police and an ambulance drew a crowd in the lane outside Agatha's house. Bill Wong was one of the first officers on the scene, and he sent a couple of his officers to persuade the onlookers to disperse. The best they could do was hold them back to allow for the arrival of more police vehicles and a doctor. Chris and Agatha were carefully examined by the doctor, as was Sayer, who was pronounced fit to be taken into custody. The crowd began to disperse when Sayer, handcuffed and escorted by two burly policemen, was driven away. The ambulance then also departed.

Agatha, Charles, Chris, and Charlotte endured hours of questions from Bill in Agatha's cottage — even a slow-motion reenactment of the living room battle — before he was satisfied that he completely understood what had happened and how Sayer had been subdued. Police officers took measurements of the scene and photographed everything from every possible angle. Eventually Bill ushered his colleagues out the door and headed back to the station for a long evening of paperwork.

"I must be off now as well," said Charles.

"Gustav is picking me up from the pub. This evening, Mary wants to set the date."

"You mean it's all still going ahead?" Agatha was astounded.

"Yes, for now . . . I mean . . . yes, it is," said Charles, holding up his hands as though to push back any further questions. "We'll talk, Aggie. Not the time or place right now."

Agatha shook her head in disbelief and Charles made for the door. Charlotte accepted his offer of a lift, promising Agatha that she would be back for her exclusive interview — an even bigger story now that she was actually part of it too. Finally Agatha and Chris were left alone.

"I'm sorry," said Chris, pointing at his bloodied shirt. "I'm in no fit state to go out for dinner, I'm afraid." He looked at his watch. "And we will definitely have lost our table."

"That's all right," Agatha said. "I can sort us out with something."

She disappeared into the kitchen and rummaged in the freezer. Minutes later, having nuked two portions of lasagne in the microwave, they were sitting opposite each other at the table.

"This isn't bad at all," Chris said, washing down a mouthful with a glass of red wine.

"And it's electric quick." Agatha smiled.

They took the remains of a bottle of Valpolicella into the living room and sat together on the sofa.

"Your poor eye," said Agatha, touching the wound where the medics had taped the cut closed. "I thought it was never going to stop bleeding."

"Cuts to the eyebrow," said Chris. "They bleed like the devil."

"And your mouth," she said. "That looks sore, too."

She leaned in and kissed him lightly on the mouth, then on the forehead. He took her face in his hands and kissed her on the lips.

"That must hurt," she said, gasping for breath.

"I'm being brave," he replied, and kissed her again, running his hands over her body. When he touched her breast, she winced.

"Ahh," she said. "Bit of a bruise there . . . Oooh . . . and down there."

She grabbed at his shirt buttons, clumsily fumbling to undo them.

"Ouch." He breathed. "Ribs . . . I . . . I don't know how this is going to work . . ."

"Don't worry," she said, pushing him slowly back onto the sofa. "I'll be gentle with you."

ABOUT THE AUTHOR

M. C. Beaton has been hailed as the "Queen of Crime" (by the Toronto *Globe and Mail*). In addition to her *New York Times* and *USA Today* bestselling Agatha Raisin novels, Beaton is the author of the Hamish Macbeth series and four Edwardian mysteries. Born in Scotland, she currently divides her time between the English Cotswolds and Paris.

The employees of Thorndike Press hope you have enjoyed this Large Print book. All our Thorndike, Wheeler, and Kennebec Large Print titles are designed for easy reading, and all our books are made to last. Other Thorndike Press Large Print books are available at your library, through selected bookstores, or directly from us.

For information about titles, please call:
  (800) 223-1244

or visit our website at:
  gale.com/thorndike

To share your comments, please write:
  Publisher
  Thorndike Press
  10 Water St., Suite 310
  Waterville, ME 04901